BLACK LEGACY PRESS™

WWW.BLACKLEGACYPRESS.ORG

Cunnie Rabbit Mr. Spider and the Other Beef

By

Florence M. Cronise

Henry W. Ward



ISBN: 978-1-63652-248-7

# CUNNIE RABBIT MR. SPIDER AND THE OTHER BEEF

FLORENCE M. CRONISE
HENRY W. WARD

# PREFACE

This little volume is sent forth with many misgivings. It claims neither literary excellence nor an entrancing theme, but professes fidelity to truth, and a desire to call attention to certain quaint and interesting phases of the inner life of a much misunderstood race.

In the compilation of these folk-lore tales, the one aim has been to make them accessible to English readers, and at the same time to retain as much as possible of their native grace and quaintness.

To accomplish this aim, the stories have been told in the dialect used by the people in their intercourse with the English, and an attempt has been made to embody the tales in a native setting with local atmosphere and colour. In addition it has seemed necessary to make a rather copious use of footnotes and explanations.

Much care has been exercised not to modify the spirit and real content of the stories. The plots and the clever little inventions are wholly native. It has seemed advisable to select only a few of the more readable stories, in the hope that they may win the sympathy of the general reader, rather than to attempt an extended collection that would discourage all but special students of folk-lore.

The stories themselves possess much intrinsic merit; if they fail to enlist the reader, the fault must be ascribed to the compilers.

The sole credit for discovering and collecting the stories is due to Miss Cronise; the arrangements of the stories here presented, and their setting, have been largely the work of Mr. Ward.

The authors are under many obligations to Mr. Alfred Sumner, a native African now in this country at college, whose intimate acquaintance with the life and customs of his people proved most helpful; also to Rev. D. F. Wilberforce, a native missionary, who has long been interested in the oral literature of his country, and in consequence has been able to give us suggestions of unusual value. To Miss Minnie Eaton of Moyamba Mission, and to other friends, who spared no pains to place desired information within our reach, and especially to the Mission boys and girls in Africa whose sympathetic interest made this collection a possibility, the gratitude of the authors is due.

**Florence M. Cronise.**

**Henry W. Ward.**

# CONTENTS

# INTRODUCTION

The collection of folk-lore tales, from which the stories contained in the present volume have been selected, was made by Miss Cronise while a teacher in the mission school at Rotifunk, Protectorate of Sierra Leone, West Africa; a mission under the control of the Woman's Board of the United Brethren Church.

The stories were collected without the remotest thought of offering them for publication. The first motive was a desire to enter more intimately into the life and mental habits of the people whom she was to instruct. This motive was soon reinforced by the attractiveness of the stories themselves, and by the fascinating manner in which they were told.

The tales were gathered from the mission children, most of whom had been brought from native homes farther inland, and from adult employees of the mission who had been long enough in contact with these white people to be found worthy of entire confidence, and to give their confidence in return.

Notwithstanding the many touches of English influence noticeable in the stories, it is believed that the ones here presented are, in all essentials, characteristically native. The same stories were heard from different persons, under different circumstances, and with every evidence of their being the spontaneous outflow of traditional lore. Sometimes a tale already heard in detail from an adult, would be told in mere outline by some child fresh from a hut of the forest.

A year or more had been spent among these people before it was discovered that they possessed a distinct oral literature, and considerably more time passed before any attempt was made to collect and record it.

Missionaries had been in this section for fifty years, but being wholly absorbed in more serious concerns, they were either unaware of this native literature, or more probably looked upon it as a part of the heathen superstition which they felt called upon to obliterate.

No one at all familiar with folk-lore, will need to be told of the peculiar difficulties experienced in making the present collection. Natives are instinctively suspicious of foreigners, and uneasy in their presence, and not only must this natural barrier be broken down, but there must spring up mutual understanding and sympathy, and outward environments must be congenial before there can be any satisfactory story-telling. The collection was made as opportunity offered, after other duties were performed. Various devices had to be resorted to, the commonest being to offer some attractive little inducement to a child of the mission or adjacent town. The child, curled up on the floor, or perched on any convenient object, would at once evince the most sympathetic interest, and then it would be a simple matter to draw out stories heard in the native wilds. By rapid writing, so abbreviated as to approach shorthand, the narratives were taken down literally, word for word. Then again, familiarity made it possible to sit near a group of children gathered in the evening for talk and laughter, and there to overhear the conundrums they propounded, and the stories they related to one another. Sometimes an adult could be induced to relate stories for an evening. One such story was a portion of a loosely connected narrative, the whole of which would occupy the evenings of an entire week.

Two years of patient endeavor brought to light one hundred

and twenty-five distinct stories. There was positive assurance of unnumbered more being current among the people, and evidence was occasionally found of the existence of another class of stories, such as the missionary would not care to hear or to record.

It may be, then, that while the fables here given truthfully reflect the life of the people, they do not reflect the whole life, but only the better, purer part.

Strangely enough, during all the years that the English have been in possession of West Africa, no one has taken the pains to collect any considerable part of the oral literature that is particularly abundant there. So far as we have been able to learn, practically nothing has been done in all the Sierra Leone region, toward collecting and publishing this great body of traditional literature. Schlenker included seven tales in his "Temne Traditions" published in 1861, and an occasional "Nancy Story" has appeared in Sierra Leone newspapers, but no serious effort has been made toward a collection; and yet perhaps no region of Africa is richer in native literature.

How completely this literature envelops the life of the people, may be inferred from the fact that the youngest children in the mission were found to possess the salient features of many stories, which they must have acquired before being taken from their people.

These stories seem to be the chief source of entertainment, not only of the young, but of the adult as well. The children of all races are fond of fables and fairy-tales, and the black man in his native state is always a child.

Whatever the distant origin of these legends and fables, it is plain that they now serve as a pleasing diversion for leisure hours, and gratify the natural hunger of the human mind for representations of its own desires as realized, without being hampered by literal fact. They fill even a larger place in the mental and ideal life of these unlettered people, than the great mass of fictitious literature does among more cultured races. There are many close parallels between this native literature and fiction as it is found among civilized peoples. Both allow a delightful freedom to the genius of the story-teller—though the imagination of the African is representative rather than creative,—both please by depicting some form of ideal achievement, both make frequent appeals to the humorous and pathetic in experience, and both furnish entertainment for hours of idleness, or offer the soul an ideal refuge from life's hard and stern realities.

Among the Africans, story-telling is mainly a pastime. It flourishes only under congenial environments and favoring conditions. These are abundant leisure, a company of sympathizing listeners, and freedom from excitement.

Story-telling most often springs spontaneously from the chat, when a number of persons are together with nothing particular to do; sometimes, however, time and place are appointed. Stories may be told whenever circumstances are favorable, but as conditions are most inviting when darkness is in possession of the outer world, most of the story-telling takes place at night. If the moon shines, its light is sufficient; should the night be dark or chill, fires are kindled, and in the flickering light of these, picturesque groups of natives may be seen, brought together by some impulse which they do not stop to question. Before the group breaks up, stories are quite likely to be started, and naturally one will draw out another, each furnishing the inspiration and the excuse for the next. The social instinct of the negro is very strong, and it leads him to seek the companionship of his fellows as often as possible. Crowded together in village communities, with few and irregular demands upon their time, and with instinctive hospitality and friendliness, the black tribes cultivate without conscious effort, their native traditions and fanciful literature. Any one may relate these tales, either as one is suggested to his mind, or on request of some one present; yet in many communities, there are persons so well versed in these common myths and legends, and so gifted in rehearsing them, that they are looked upon as the village story-tellers, and are expected to do most of the reciting. If the people know that a person so gifted is among them, they go and beg him for a story, offering him some present—perhaps tobacco, kola nuts, cowry shells, which are used as currency, or some other small article. Then they build a great fire and sit around it while the story is told.

We have it also on good native authority, that there are occasionally professionals who make their living by going from village to village, and exchanging for food and shelter, stories interspersed with songs. Many of these African troubadours display remarkable dramatic power. Voice, eyes, face, hands, head, and indeed the whole person aid in giving force to the words.

The reader will greatly enhance his pleasure in the perusal of the following tales, if he will give his own imagination full play, and will supply what the narrator added by the manner of his delivery.

Riddles and story-telling are not infrequently continued throughout the entire night, and in connection with an unusual occasion, such as the funeral ceremonies of some distinguished person, or the marriage festivities of a similar personage. They may be protracted for several nights.

Many little songs, or rather choruses, occur in the stories. These are rendered in a kind of chanting measure, a weird melody, usually accompanied by a rhythmical clapping of the hands. They are invariably short, usually in the minor key, and, in the longer stories, are repeated at intervals, seemingly to give variety and animation to the narrative. It makes a peculiar impression upon the distant listener to hear these periodical choruses break forth suddenly on the night air, and just as suddenly cease.

The songs are invariably given in the native language, and the crude attempt at translation given by the narrator, fails utterly to reproduce their musical qualities.

Negro folk-lore, whether in Africa or America, consists largely of animal stories, in which human qualities and characteristics are ascribed to the various animals. In the Temne legends, the Spider, the Cunning Rabbit, the Deer, the Leopard, the Turtle, the Elephant, the Lizard, the Chameleon, the Cat and the Hawk appear very frequently, while many other animals, birds and insects are introduced. It appears to be assumed, throughout the stories, that there was a time when all animals dwelt together in a single community, until some of the animals began to prey upon the others, thus scattering them over the face of the earth, creating enmities, and destroying the power to understand one another. The communities were organized with king and headmen, and had houses and farms, occupations and wants, like the men of later times.

Several accounts are given of how the animals came to be dispersed. The one contained in this collection, of Mister Spider and his powerful witch medicine, is evidently, in part at least, a late invention. It represents Spider in his usual rôle of devising some cunning scheme for securing a supply of food for himself and family. In this instance he procures a gun and ammunition, and announces that he has secured a medicine to kill off the witches that infest the town; and thus, under pretence of rendering the community a valuable service, he begins to kill and to devour the animals one by one. They finally take alarm, and flee to different parts of the earth.

Another story, bearing the marks of greater antiquity, represents the animals as living together in peace and harmony, until the Leopard develops a taste for fresh meat, and begins to prey upon the other animals. They hold a council, and finally decide to take the only boat in existence, and to remove to an island of the sea, leaving Mr. Leopard alone on the mainland. Every day some one is left to guard the boat, while the others are away procuring food. Once, while the Deer is left on guard, Leopard comes to the shore, and in a disguised voice calls for the boat to be brought across. Mr. Deer, always represented in these stories as being extremely stupid, is deceived, and rows the boat across. Of course Mr. Leopard devours the unfortunate Deer, seizes the boat and plans a general feast when the animals return to the village at night. To save themselves, they scatter in every direction, and thus animals become dispersed over the earth.

Hereafter the animals appear to have had dealings with each other, more or less, but were never again united, although there is mention of their gathering for special purposes on several occasions.

The stories frequently assume to account for the peculiar traits or physical characteristics of the various animals; as, for instance, why the Deer coughs, why the Leopard is spotted, why the Spider is flat and why his waist is small, why the Elephant's tusks protrude, and why the Turtle's shell is rough and scarred.

Certain definite qualities and characteristics are ascribed to particular animals, and to these they hold consistently through all the stories. The Deer is always stupid and helpless; the Elephant enormously strong but lacking in mental acuteness; the Cunning Rabbit intelligent and lovable; and the Spider shrewd, designing, selfish, and sometimes vindictive and cruel.

It is noticeable that the weak and helpless creatures are made to prevail against the strong and mighty, not by any use of force, but by cleverness and cunning. Thus Mr. Spider defeats both the Elephant and the Hippopotamus in a pulling match, by the clever ruse of challenging them, in turn, to a trial of strength, proposing to draw the Elephant from the shore to the water, and the Hippopotamus from the water to the shore. The Spider procures a rope so long that neither antagonist can see the other. At the appointed time he ties one end of it to the Elephant, and says that when he is ready to begin the contest, he will give the signal by shaking the rope; then going to the water's edge, he ties the other end to the Hippopotamus, giving the same instructions. Finally, going to the middle of the rope, he gives the signal, and the struggle begins, while Mr. Spider enjoys the sport from behind a tree, to which place of safety he has had the good judgment to retreat.

As the two monsters are so equally matched in strength, the struggle continues, with advantage to neither, until both are completely exhausted and fall down dead. Mr. Spider, viewing the results of his cleverness, soliloquises: "Yo' pass me fo' 'trong, but aintee I pass yo' fo' sense?"

The victims of this cunning supply food to Mr. Spider and his family throughout the famine, and that indeed was the Spider's purpose in the ruse. The story throws in the gratuitous information that the Spider cast into the water such portions of the carcasses as were not desirable for food, and from these pieces came fish, the first of their kind.

Mental superiority counts for more than mere brute force,

even where there is a direct trial of strength, as in the story of "Cunning Rabbit and his Well." The other animals come to wrestle with Cunning Rabbit for the privilege of taking water from his well, but on account of his "sense," Cunning Rabbit is always victor, even to hurling the Elephant into the air, although the latter tried to hold himself down by wrapping his trunk around a tree.

Sometimes a necromantic spell is called in to aid the weaker, as in the case of Goro, the Wrestler, in which the song of incantation chanted by the mother, enables the child to prevail.

It satisfies the ethical sense of all people, to represent helpless innocence as finally triumphant over the selfish power of might. Perhaps the black race has more than usual reason for representing in its imaginative literature, that cunning, craft and cleverness are the qualities most to be admired and cultivated. It has always been an oppressed people, defenceless in the contest with wild beasts, without adequate resources in the struggle with nature, and helpless against the cruelties of their more aggressive fellowmen. Little wonder that they exalt cunning, deception and craft. If there is a dash of viciousness in these, all the better. It is only poetic retribution. Consequently the African is taught dissimulation as a fine art, and cunning as the most worthy of accomplishments.

The Spider appears to be the national hero, the impersonation of the genius of the race. To him are ascribed the qualities most characteristic of the people, or those most to be desired: cunning, sleeplessness, almost immortality, an unlimited capacity for eating, and an equal genius for procuring the necessary supplies. He possesses a charmed life, and escapes from all intrigue. He is a tireless weaver, and has spun the thread of his personality into all the warp and woof of the national life. With him the adults associate most of their traditions, while the children love him, and push him tenderly aside if he chances to come in their way. He is inclined to be lazy, and refuses to lift even the lightest burden if it is in the nature of work; if it is something to eat, he can carry the carcass of an elephant with the greatest ease.

The Spider occupies the same place in the folk-lore of West Africa, as does Brer Rabbit in the tales of the southern negro, and as Annancy holds among the negroes of the West Indies, or Hlakanyana among the Kaffirs of South Africa. A comparative study of these several heroes and the literature gathered about them, would be extremely interesting and profitable, but would carry us beyond the bounds set for this introduction.

Mr. Harris, in his introduction to "Nights With Uncle Remus," has pointed out the essential identity of Brer Rabbit and Hlakanyana. There is perhaps a closer parallel between the Spider of the Temne tales, and Annancy, the hero of the West Indian stories. A comparison of Mr. Spider and Brer Rabbit reveals many similarities and some differences, the latter due no doubt to the mellowing influence of contact with a finer civilization, an influence that has softened the character of the transplanted negro, and wrought the same change in the hero of his stories. Both are exceedingly clever, and equal to any emergency. Brer Rabbit, however, is inoffensive in his mischief, and very properly gets out of every scrape without serious consequences. If ever he gets others into trouble, it is to save himself, or to settle an old score. Mr. Spider's cunning has at times a touch of viciousness in it. It sometimes overreaches itself, and brings Mr. Spider to grief, though never to destruction.

Cunning Rabbit rivals Mr. Spider in shrewdness and wit, and in the reverence and esteem given him by the people. In pure intelligence and in amiability of disposition he is without a peer. He is uniformly pronounced "King of de beef fo' wise, oh!" He and Mr. Spider are usually on amicable terms, but when their interests clash there is a notable contest of wits. The natives say: "Two cunnie meet up, de one cunnie, de odder cunnie," but Cunning Rabbit always has a shade the better of it in the end.

We have found it very difficult to identify this little creature, called by the natives "Cunnie Rabbit." It is evidently not a rabbit at all, but the water deerlet or chevrotain, noted for its nimbleness and cunning. It is about eighteen inches long, slender and graceful in form, with a soft fawn-colored skin, and the daintiest of legs and feet. The little creature is very difficult to secure. Its shyness, fleetness and cunning have led the natives to invest it with a sort of veneration.

A fragment of skeleton submitted to Dr. F. W. True, Head Curator Department of Biology, Smithsonian Institution, was pronounced to belong to Hyomoschus Aquaticus, an animal peculiar to West Africa.

It would be the merest conjecture to surmise that this water deerlet, the Cunning Rabbit of African folk-lore, may be the ancestor of Brer Rabbit, as the negroes of the South portray him, and yet there is a shadow of evidence for such belief. The negroes might have transferred the qualities of their Cunning Rabbit to the American hare, because of the similarity of their popular names. It certainly requires a very friendly eye to see in the hare all the mental acumen accredited by the negroes to Brer Rabbit.

To students of comparative folk-lore, these little stories will furnish much food for reflection. They probably come as nearly fresh from the hearts of a primitive people, and are as little modified by outside influences, as any collection made in recent times.

To the oft-repeated question as to how the story was learned, and whence it came, the uniform answer was: "Oh, please, Missus, f'om *f-a-r* up country," with a much prolonged emphasis on the "far," and an intonation that expressed wonder at such a question's being asked, as all such stories must come from the infinitely remote in space and time.

It will be observed that very many of the stories in this collection are almost identical with a number of the tales in the "Uncle Remus" series, and with a few in the "Annancy Stories," to say nothing of likenesses found in the folk-lore of the American Indians, and the very natural similarity between these tales and those current among the negroes of other portions of Africa.

The "Tar Baby" story, which seems to be in the oral literature of all African tribes, and a standard among the folk-lore tales of all peoples, appears here as the "Wax Girl."

The incidents leading up to the encounter of Mr. Spider with the Wax Girl, differ from the preliminaries in the story of Brer Rabbit and the Tar Baby, but the encounter itself is the same in both. The outcome also differs in the two stories, but in each is entirely consistent with the story as a whole. Brer Rabbit has been guilty of no offence that deserves punishment, so he suffers only temporary humiliation, and finally regains simultaneously his freedom and his prestige, by inducing Mr. Fox to fling him into the brier patch. Mr. Spider, on the other hand, has practised gross deception, and has appropriated to his own use what should have been shared with others, so he very appropriately receives as punishment an unmerciful flogging at the hands of the outraged community.

Mr. Spider's feat of strength in his contest with the Elephant and the Hippopotamus, already referred to, is a variant of the same contest between Mr. Terrapin and Mr. Bear.

The Temne story of the Turtle making a riding-horse of Mr. Leopard, finds its parallel in Brer Rabbit's riding Brer Fox, as told by "Uncle Remus," and in the "Annancy Stories," by Pamela Colman Smith, where Annancy rides the Tiger.

In one instance Mr. Leopard feigns death, and when the other animals gather around to wail for him, he seizes and devours them. This is much like Mr. Wildcat's attempt to secure the wild turkey by the same ruse.

It must suffice to have mentioned a few variants only, although there are many more of the same nature. If anything further were needed to prove that the folk-tales of the American negroes were brought with them from Africa, the striking parallels in the tales of the two countries ought to supply the proof.

The magic nuts, or eggs, or other articles, which appear in the folk-lore of most races, and which on being opened let out, at one time a profusion of all things desired—riches, fine houses, servants etc., and at other times, reptiles, insects, and cruel monsters, are also found among these tales. The story of the devil's magic eggs is a representative of this class. In another story the bangah-nuts take the place of the eggs.

There are also traces of the "half thing" conception. In one story a man's possessions consisted of half things of various kinds, a half pot, a half bowl, everything half. A bird that possessed magic power, befriended the poor man, and transformed the "bush" into a village filled with riches, to be his on condition of never disturbing the bird's egg. The condition is finally violated, and the man, made utterly destitute, learns that half a thing is better than none. In the story contained in this collection, in which a young girl marries a devil, it will be noted that the devil in taking human form, was compelled to supply his hideous deficiency by borrowing half a head, one foot, one hand, everything half; and after his successful wooing, when he approached his own home, with his bride, all the half things that he had borrowed fell off one by one, until finally "all t'ing nah heen skin bin lef half."

In all the stories we possess, there is only one mention of the divining mirror. It is employed by a lover, and startles him by revealing his loved one lying dead.

It may aid the reader to appreciate these fables from Temne-Land, if a few paragraphs of this introduction be given to a brief discussion of the peculiar beliefs, customs, and environments of the people who have formulated the stories, and who repeat them with never-dying interest.

If we could get a true and complete picture of the black man's mental and moral world from his view point, we should be able to confer a measureless boon upon all those who must deal with him; but unfortunately we have no such good gift to offer. The negro character is so perverse and enigmatical that it defies satisfactory analysis.

The stories themselves will furnish the best kind of information on these points, and to the serious student, this perhaps will be their chief value. However a summary of a few of the facts available will not be amiss. What is said, though applicable directly to the Temnes, will be true in a general sense of all the surrounding tribes, and in a limited way of all the race. As a people, the Temnes are filled exceedingly with innate pride and natural dignity, and love to be noticed and honored. They are fond of riches as they understand them, and are shrewd traders. Their wealth consists of wives, slaves, cows, and goats, and these they value in the order named. Mentally they are bright and quick-witted, though only as concerns the reproductive powers of the mind; for independent thinking they have little capacity. The memory powers are especially strong and persistent. The black man keeps in his head records that a white man would be compelled to write in a book.

The native African has few ambitions beyond the satisfying of his appetites, and the gratification of his sensual desires. Contentment with his lot is the bane of his life, so far as any hope of improvement is concerned, and yet these stories reveal glimmerings of better things, and a capacity to formulate ideals. It is not an easy matter to know the impulses that lie deep within the breast of any people,—the central life impulses, out of which flow all desires and motives, and all standards of happiness. It is still more difficult to get at this central impulse in an uncivilized people, because heathenism renders the soul-life of its adherents extremely difficult to understand.

The literature of a people is the best revelation of its soul-life, especially of the ideals it would consciously or unconsciously set up. It is in this fact that such collections as the one here offered, find their greatest worth.

The inner life of the African is so completely under the control of his superstitious beliefs, that to comprehend it adequately, one must understand all the hideous network of superstitions that envelop the whole life of the people.

Mr. Alfred Sumner, an educated native, has kindly furnished us the following facts concerning this phase of the life of his people.

"All the people believe in signs and omens, good and bad; every occurrence that is a little beyond the ordinary, or seems a little strange, must receive some interpretation from the natives. In fact, occurrences that are not beyond the natural, so long as they do not happen every day, are the sign of something. The withering of a tree, the falling of a fence, the stumbling against something in the road, the ringing of the ear, the dancing of the eyelid, the itching palm, two babies laughing at each other; these and many more things that time would fail us to mention, mean something to the native; tokens of good, warnings of calamity near. The cry of the witch bird, and the "cluck, cluck, cluck" of the boa-constrictor, mean the certain death of someone. If one should be killed by lightning on the road, persons passing the spot from that time on, must pluck a leaf or a small branch and throw it there to avert the same death. Some parts of a road have been entirely abandoned and new paths made on this account. One dare not sew his cloth while it is on his body, lest a relative of his die. There are many more, to us silly superstitions, in which the natives fully believe. To them they are signs and wonders. Some are easy to interpret, others must come under the prophetic eye of the "country-fashion" man—a man who interprets signs and wonders either by spiritual means, or on sand, or with stones. All sorts of charms are made and worn. Various articles are used in their composition—such as oil, leaves, beads, hair, finger-nails, toe-nails etc. Most of the charms the women put on in Africa, are merely small bits of paper with Mohammedan writing, wrapped in a piece of soft leather. They are either to ward off evil, or to bring about luck, according to the writing on the paper. All the "Sebbehs"—that is, the flat, regularly formed charms—are made in this way. Not all of the charms are to be seen by everybody; some are very private, and must be worn next the skin. The "hoodoos" and "fetiches" are of more importance than the ordinary charms, and their composition is more complex, consisting of leaves, barks, roots, horns and bones, either of man or beast, or of both, all carefully placed in a country-pot made of clay, and kept from every eye save that of the owners and perhaps near relatives. These fetiches may serve as gods, and are believed to have the power to return evil for evil to any one who may harm their owners. What is called "gree-gree" is a fetich that is employed by its owner to revenge any wrong received by him. The "He-ge-de" is considered to have the power of self-motion, and of attacking in a death-combat the one to whom it is sent. These charms may be used by any one, irrespective of rank or age; but some of them are very costly, and only the rich can afford them. The leopard's teeth are considered very great and valuable ornaments—pearls of great price; and natives are loth to sell them. They may well be called their diamonds, as they not infrequently calculate their wealth by the number of leopard's teeth owned."

It is thus seen that the natives are born, reared, and die in nameless terror of unseen powers that teem in woods, fields and towns. Their spirits are legion. A few of these are believed to be good, the majority bad, exceedingly bad. It is the greater part of their existence to circumvent the evil spirits, and to win the favor of the good. The tiniest babe is decorated with strings, shells, or bits of wood, supposed to possess the power to ward off evils which mother-arms cannot avert. Those of maturer years, even down to old age, often sacrifice to conciliate they know not what.

Sickness is believed to be caused by a witch. If one is seized with serious illness, a witch-doctor is called in to exorcise the evil spirit; failing in thus obtaining relief, the next resort is to incantations and ordeals, to discover who is guilty of bewitching the afflicted one, some individual being held guilty of bringing on the malady.

The power of the witch-doctor is considered absolute, and woe to the unfortunate one that falls under his ill-will. He is believed to possess the power of double vision, and to be able to see spirits, and to know their doings. Never is the power and efficiency of his incantations doubted. His exorbitant fees are paid with a cheerfulness that would quite astound a Christian doctor. A curse pronounced in the name of a witch-medicine is supposed to be relentless towards the one against whom it is directed. The following is a good example of a native curse.

"Oh, thou medicine, the person who stole this my rice, cloth, lamp, fruit, bed, or pot, I give this person into your hands. If you leave this person you leave your fowl (used in sacrifice). I swear the person's lungs, heart and liver. If the person goes to work, let him cut himself, and if he goes to war let him be killed; everything he does, let evil come upon him."

The "Country-fashion" man, also, is supposed to possess the power of double vision, but of a slightly different kind. He can see the mysterious occult powers that operate beyond the reach of ordinary vision. He is therefore prophet and seer, the interpreter of signs and omens, and various mysterious occurrences.

In the social relations of the people, a loose caste system prevails, based chiefly upon might. The chief exacts obedience and service from all beneath him. Men make servants of women, and of other weaker men. In a polygamous household, the head wife regards the other wives as her inferiors and servants, while each wife makes practical slaves of her own children. The older children in turn exact service of the younger. He is poor indeed, who cannot find another weaker than himself to do his bidding. Society is a pyramid with the weakest at the bottom, and the strongest at the top.

It remains to make the necessary explanations of the dialect of the stories, and with that this introduction must close.

The general reader may feel like protesting against the use of a dialect that presents so many difficulties, and the philologist will object to the form employed, as being too much influenced by English associations to represent the dialect of the people in its native purity.

To both classes of readers our apology may seem weak and inadequate. In the first place, the stories would lose much of their vitality and force if the flavor of the peculiar mental qualities of the people who tell them should be lost by an attempt at translation. The ideal means of expression would be the vigorous and picturesque native tongue, did it not exclude all but the initiated from sharing the stories. The next best thing is to allow the native mind to express itself in its own adaptation of a foreign language.

As to the form the dialect has been allowed to take, it may be said that it differs from that used by the people in daily conversation, only as formal English differs from the colloquial. There is a little nearer approach to subordination of clauses than is found in ordinary conversation, and a larger per cent of English words is employed, as might be expected from those who have had some training in that language. This necessarily involves an inconsistency, inasmuch as the stories are represented as being told by natives in their native environment; but as the whole undertaking has presented peculiar difficulties, some degree of allowance may be expected.

The dialect is that of the Temne people, and is essentially the dialect of Sierra Leone, from which it was derived. Each new tribe, in learning the dialect, modified it slightly, so that, although it is perfectly intelligible to all the tribes using it, an attempt to represent the words phonetically, reveals many differences. Wherever the pronunciation of common words, such as "make," "take," "come" etc., very closely approximates the English usage, we have not hesitated to give the correct English form.

The whole dialect is a hopeless jumble of English and African words. It is very much condensed, almost stenographic in its brevity, and requires the aid of voice and gesture to round it out to like-life fulness. This requirement, the native temperament, being emotional and picturesque, meets to perfection. These accessories the imagination of the reader must supply, if he is to receive the keenest pleasure from the perusal of the stories.

With the native, a common device of expression is the repetition of the emphatic word or phrase, or else its very much prolonged utterance. The word "Sotáy"—accent on the last syllable—when used in the sense of "a long time," is prolonged until the very utterance conveys the impression desired. Naturally, the vocabulary is very meager. There are no words to express shades of meaning. Every thing that in any way pleases the eye is "fine." Every thing that pleases the taste, either literally or figuratively, is "sweet." Rice is "sweet," pepper is "sweet," and fighting is "sweet." Gender is ignored. "He" stands for "he," "she," or "it," indiscriminately. "Me Mammy he go bring yo' him son Mary, to-morrow." Idea of number is rudimentary. "He" is uniformly singular, and "dem" is usually plural. "Um" occurs often in the objective singular, but the variation in number appears to be purely accidental. "Dey" is rarely used for the pronoun "they," although to avoid confusion it has been allowed to appear quite frequently in the stories. "Dem" and "den" are used interchangeably for "they," and since there is no distinction in case, they may also be used for them. "Den" is seldom used for "then," but is usually a pronoun. The reader will need to exercise special care on this point. For the adverb "there," the natives invariably use "deh." There is a peculiar use of an auxiliary that will need careful notice. Its sound is between that of "dey" and "duh;" the latter has been chosen. "He duh come" means "He is coming," or "He comes," in the historical present. However, laws of language are trampled on with utmost unconcern. "Go" is used occasionally as a sign of the future. "He go come" meaning "he will come," and "he go go," "he will go." Certain words are repeated to form a single expression, as "so-so," meaning "merely," "nothing but." "San'-san'" is sand, and "bug-a-bug" is the white ant. Idiomatic expressions occur frequently, and unless mastered at once, may prove confusing; once understood, they are very expressive. "He no tay" means "it does not stay," that is, Time does not linger, or, It is but a short time. "Pass" is used in all comparisons, in the sense of surpass, excel, exceed, etc.; as—"Spider pass Elephan' fo' sense," "I pass yo' fo' 'trong." "Pull" is employed in the peculiar sense of "produce," "devise," "create," as: "He pull one big holler," "He pull dis sense," "God pull de people," referring to the creation of Adam and Eve. "No mo'" is an expression frequently found, and although no single English expression can cover the meaning in all of its uses, it signifies "only that and nothing more." "He de one man no mo'" means "only he and no one else." "So-so san'-san' no mo'," "entirely sand, nothing more."

But of these expressions there are not many, so the difficulty in mastering them will not be great. It has often been difficult to find a spelling that represents correctly the sound desired. The natives never say "house," but always "ho'se," giving "s" its sibilant sound. With the further aid of the vocabulary printed at the end of the volume, there should be little difficulty in reading the stories.

It may be said in conclusion, that no one can be more conscious of the fragmentary nature of the literature presented in this volume, or of the faulty manner of its presentation, than are the authors themselves.

**F. M. C.**

**H. W. W.**

*Toledo, Iowa.*

## CHAPTER I

# WHEN THE NIGHT HAS COME

The African day was lingering for a brief moment in a tropical twilight, as if reluctant to give over a world of natural beauty to the impenetrable darkness of a moonless, forest night. The mud huts of the native village, with their conical, palm-thatched roofs, showed in the fading twilight like great shocks of harvested grain in a little field fenced in by a high hedge of trees. Narrow foot-paths—the only suggestion of streets—wound irregularly through the village, and in these, children, innocently nude, were romping, and chasing each other with all the noisy delight of that care-free age. Men and women, led by their inclination to gossip, or by an instinctive shrinking from the gathering darkness, were unconsciously drifting into groups about fires that had been kindled here and there in the irregular open spaces. Other light the village had none, and the little fires seemed only to exaggerate the thick curtain of gloom that was now drawing around the place. The countless invisible and mysterious forces that control the destiny of the unfortunate black man, seemed to be taking on bodily shapes, and to be stealing forth under cover of the night to work their spells through forest and earth and air. Out of the stilly darkness came myriad voices of the night—familiar ones from within the village, the explosive chant and monotonous beat of the drum that accompanied a weird tribal dance, or the shouts of irrepressible childhood still at play, or more often the hum of conversation that told of the sway of gossip, or the fascination of myth and story. Anon came the awesome, half-terrifying voices from the outer night—the uncanny insect chorus, or the distant call of wild beasts, speaking to one another a language that seemed full of meaning, but which the human ear had lost the power to understand.

To-night the voices possessed a peculiar fascination for the group gathered around Sobah's fire. Coarse banter and desultory gossip had ceased to interest; the spirit of the night was upon them, and the voices from the darkness seemed to address them personally, and to assert the kinship of all creatures. It scarcely needed the accumulated traditions of untold generations to convince these listeners that their ancestors had once possessed the ability to comprehend their fellow-creatures, and so had dwelt on terms of equality and friendship with them. As it was, Sobah and his friends did not trouble themselves about beliefs, but in imagination passed easily and naturally into that realm where all creatures spoke a common language, and possessed common needs and attributes.

For some time Sobah had been sitting in silence, wholly absorbed in his own mental processes. Suddenly an inspiration seemed to stir him. He tossed back his head, his eyes began to sparkle, and his face to glow with the anticipated delight of the story that had come to him from the depths of his capacious memory. These significant preliminaries were quickly noted. "He duh get story," was the warning exclamation passed around the group. Every eye was at once riveted upon Sobah's face, and every countenance took on a look of eager expectancy.

Konah, a bright-eyed, ebony-hued beauty of thirteen years, who all her life had seemed to possess the supernatural power of being present unnoted whenever anything new or marvellous was to be seen or heard, came up just at this moment, led by unerring instinct, and settled down unobserved in the shadow, ready to absorb every word.

Casting a dignified glance around the company, to assure himself that all were properly attentive, Sobah proceeded to relate the wonderful exploits of Mr. Spider, in meeting the requirements of his prospective mother-in-law.

## Mr. Spider Wins A Wife

"One ooman get girl pickin (pickaninny). Dis girl done do fo' married, but no man no deh (there) wey (who) able fo' married um, because de mammy no 'gree. Well, Spider come, he say he go married de girl, en de mammy answer um, say:

"'Yo' mus' fus' do dis t'ree t'ing; bring Lion teet' wey fresh wid blood 'pon um, en sass-wood palm-wine, en bowman'" (boa-constrictor).

Here the story was interrupted by a chorus of "Eh! eh's!" and other exclamations of wonder at the impossibility of each of the three conditions imposed.

"Lion 'trong too much," protested Dogbah, who was sadly wanting in the imaginative quality, and demanded hard, prosaic fact, "Spider no able fo' get heen teet' fresh wid blood 'pon um."

Gondomah, who was of a rather silent and thoughtful turn, said meditatively, as if speaking to himself:

"Palm-tree no get banana, sass-wood no get palm-wine." It was his way of asserting the impossibility of securing palm-wine from the poisonous sass-wood.

"Spider leelee (little) too much fo' bring big, big bowman," was the verdict of Oleemah, and yet his tone contradicted his words.

Sobah silenced the interruptions with the pertinent question: "Aintee Spider pass all fo' cunnie? He able fo' do um." Then he proceeded:

"Spider say he go try fo' all dem t'ing fo' get de girl. He go inside one big forest wey (where) all de beef (animals) duh (do) pass. He make leelee fiah by de road. De part wey de smoke duh go he make good bench, so de beef kin sit down. He say: Make dem come wa'm fiah,[1] de cole too much, because nar (it is) rainy season. He say make dem no come togedder, make dem come one one. He kare (carried) one hammer, heaby one, wey he fo' hole wid two han'. He hide um. Well, den beef all duh come. De' one he no wan' he no hit um, he jus' duh coax, make dem go get de big beef fo' come. Well, w'en den beef all done come, w'en dey duh wa'm fiah, dey go call Lion fo' say: 'Eh! Spider one good man, dis make he duh make good fiah fo' we en we cumpin (companions).'

"Well, one day Lion come, en Spider he make de smoke good fashion; put plenty leaf deh. W'en Lion come he say:

"'Fren', I sorry fo' dah cole wey ketch yo'. Kahbo (welcome)! All day I duh make good fiah fo' yo'.'

"Well, he go wipe de bench good fashion, he say, make Lion sit down fo' wa'm fiah. De Lion sit down. Spider take mo' leaf, raw one, fo' make smoke come out *plenty*. Dis yeah big smoke go 'pon Lion; he shut he yi, he duh open he teet', he duh wa'm hese'f; he no know say Spider duh watch um fo' hit um wid hammer 'pon heen teet'. Spider take de hammer soffle (softly), he hit Lion *one* tem, no mo', but dah hit wey he *hit* um! Lion he pull one big, big holler tay (until) all de groun' duh shake. He spit heen teet' out 'pon de groun', he run!"

Sobah had been telling his story with voice, countenance, hands and suggestive motions of his whole body, and as the climax approached, his impressiveness increased. The hearers were shaking with suppressed mirth, and when they saw the result of Spider's cunning, and Lion beating an ignominious retreat, leaving his teeth behind him, they could restrain the inevitable outburst of laughter no longer. Some of the more excitable threw themselves upon the ground in an ecstasy of delight. Konah had become so identified with her favorite, Mr. Spider, and was so pleased with his success, that she forgot her own art of cunning, and crept boldly out of the shadow.

Sobah chuckled contentedly, while the outburst was expending itself, then went on.

"Spider hese'f run, he mean say de Lion go grip um. W'en he see Lion no duh follow, he turn back, he take de teet', he kare um go to de ooman, he say:

"'Look me, I done bring dah raw lion teet' wid de blood.'"

"De ooman say: 'All ret, but he lef' mo' t'ing fo' do. Go bring dah sass-wood palm-wine.'

"Spider come out, he take heen ax, he sharp um, "Wahtah, wootah! wahtah, wootah!"[2] He fine one sass-wood 'tick (tree), he klim 'pon um, he dig hole, he come down. He go buy country-pot, big pot, he tie big rope 'pon um, make um 'trong; ef he no 'trong bimeby de pot go fa' down, he broke, because palm-wine go full um. W'en he done hang um he no sleep all net, he go 'roun' to den people all, he tief (steals) plenty palm-wine, he trow um 'way (empties it) inside de pot wey hang to dah dry sass-wood 'tick, en he full dis pot wid de people yown palm-wine[3] sotay he t'row 'way' nah groun'. He duh rub palm-wine inside de hole, en 'pon de 'tick all. He tell one man say:

"'Make yo' follow me, look ef de palm-wine run.'"

"Spider takes the hammer soffle."

This bit of shrewdness on the part of Mr. Spider, Sobah unfolded with intensest appreciation in tone and gesture, and was rewarded at this point with grunts of satisfaction and approval from the listeners, and with exclamations of unbounded admiration for the clever little hero who could both steal and deceive without detection. As soon as the silence told him they were ready for more, he proceeded.

"W'en dey go, dey meet de pot full. Spider tell heen cumpin fo' take um down, en dey two dey tote um sotay (until) dey reach de ole ooman. Spider pin (place) um down 'pon de groun', he say:

"'Mammy, look dah sass-wood palm-wine!'

"De ooman ax de man: 'Nar true?'

"He say: 'Yes, nar me see um wid me yown yi.'

"Well de ooman say:

"'Odder t'ing lef' yet fo' do befo' I gie yo' me pickin. Go bring live Bowman.'

"Spider go nah puttah-puttah,[4] he look sotay (until) he jus' meet Bowman, he say:

"'Fren', how do?'

"Bowman answer um: 'Tankee!'

"Spider kare one long 'tick, big one, he say:

"'One day me bin say Bowman long pass dis 'tick, but me cumpin done deny, dey say: "No, he no kin pass um fo' long." Make yo' lie down 'pon de 'tick fo' try ef yo' pass de 'tick fo' long, or de 'tick pass yo'.'

"Well, Bowman lie down; Spider take leelee rope, he begin fo' tie Bowman to heen neck, he say:

"'Nar play I duh play.[5] No make palaver, nar so I go tie yo' fo' make yo' no ben' ben' any place, fo' make yo' lie 'traight 'pon dis 'tick.'

"Bowman 'gree; he lie down soffle. Spider no tie um 'trong, he jus' tie um leelee tay he reach de tail side. He go back to de head, he draw de rope tight, he say:

"'Aintee I bin tell yo' nar play I duh play? I kare yo' fo' go to dem plenty people, fo' make den no deny me agin.'

"W'en Spider finish fo' tie um, Bowman no get 'trenk (strength),[6] betty no dey agin fo' um. Spider tote um, he go gie um to dah mammy, he mudder-in-law. W'en de ooman see Spider done bring Bowman, he call plenty people, dey talk de palaver, dey say Spider do well, make de mammy gie um de girl fo' married, en he gie um. Nar so Spider do fo' he wef."

Cold type does scant justice to the sympathetic tone and expressive movements with which the story was told, or to the low chuckling laugh with which its finer points were enforced.

Gratified by the pleasure his story had given, Sobah was content to rest for the present, and after listening respectfully for some time to his less gifted companions, left the group and disappeared within his hut.

As the inclination seized them, the others strolled away into the darkness. Careful Mammy Mamenah covered the fire, and soon the night was given over to the undisputed possession of spirits and other creatures of darkness.

## CHAPTER II

# WITH THE SPIRITS OF THE WOOD

When one morning, not long after the story of Mr. Spider's successful courting, Sobah felt the hunter instinct strong upon him, he left the work of the little rice farm to Mammy Mamenah and some pickaninnies, took his trusted hunting-spear and sought the forest depths. He was a knowing hunter, artful and sure, and as familiar with the ways of the denizens of the woods as with the habits of his village neighbors.

But through all the morning hours his skill and cunning proved of no avail. He sought the well-known haunts of the desired prey, and lay patiently in wait, or followed a fresh trail, with every faculty alert. All in vain, for the spirits of the forest seemed in league against him. Always some unseen presence would give warning of his approach, or bewitch his aim. Tired out at last, and full of nameless dread, he threw himself down at the foot of a monkey-apple tree to think out the mystery. The cough of a deer from a neighboring thicket seemed to taunt his ill-success. A monkey swung down from a limb over his head, and chattered threateningly. A heavy body seemed to fall through the branches of a tree just behind him, and yet, as he turned, no object falling was visible. Starting up with the cry, "Now debble dat!" Sobah reached instinctively for the charm he always wore on his person as a safeguard against danger and an assurance of success. To his consternation he discovered that it was not in its accustomed place. The cause of his former ill-luck was now explained. This charm contained a potent medicine brought from afar, and had been consecrated as his personal guardian and helper. Greatly wrought up now at finding himself in this devil-haunted region without a charm so powerful, he made his way from the woods and to his hut with eager haste. To his great relief he found the precious little article hanging where he had carelessly left it. Much reassured when this object of his superstitious trust was again dangling from his neck, he started out once more, and in a new direction, bent on retrieving his lost prestige as a hunter. Sustained by that feeling of confidence which is half of success in any undertaking, he, keen-eyed and alert, followed the path along the river. Sagaciously hiding in a covert that overlooked a little path leading down to the water's edge, he awaited developments. A little later his quick ear detected the lightest possible step approaching along the path; then a pair of intelligent eyes peeped around a tuft of rushes, and soon there appeared the most graceful little body Nature ever made, incased in a glossy coat of softest satin, and supported by the daintiest of feet. Even in repose the little creature suggested the very poetry of motion, and looked as if the working of a slight spell would transform it wholly into spirit and let it fly away.

Sobah's heart had been nurtured in savagery, yet it almost stayed the hand from striking.

"Cunnie Rabbit," he muttered to himself, for so the natives call this deerlet, "I go get yo' now."

Surely the charm was working, for there the shy creature stood, and moved not until the well-directed spear from the hunter's hand laid it low.

While Sobah was gloating over his prize, a company of men from the village came along. After effusive congratulations, they tied Cunnie Rabbit upon a pole, covered the body with a white cloth, and eight men took up the burden and staggered along toward the village with it, as if the load were all they could possibly carry. "Eight man tote um," Mamenah explained later to the inquisitive Konah, "dem duh make as ef he heaby. Dey say he nar (is) king of de beas' fo' wise oh; not fo' stout, but fo' sense."

The stew that accompanied the usual boiled rice at that evening meal, was delicious enough to please a more fastidious palate.

With appetite richly satisfied for once, and in great good humor with himself and the world, Sobah was in a more genial mood than usual, when, later, a company of neighbors gathered around him. They had just come in from their little farms, and, remembering similar occasions, and knowing that if the hunter had been successful in the chase, his tongue would be "sweet" for story-telling, each man carried on his back a bundle of wood. Throwing it in a heap suggestive of a fire, they remarked: "Lookee de wood fo' de fiah," thus making a covert request for a story, and paying the story-teller a delicate compliment. Sobah felt the beauty of this indirect appeal, and was much pleased by it, but there was no need for haste, so he allowed the talk to run on various topics before he made a formal response to the desire of his friends.

All chatted freely of the experiences of the day. A bit of war news from "up country" had drifted in, and was heard with relish. Most of all the behavior of the various animals Sobah had met that day, and the supposed connection between the little charm and that behavior, held awed attention. Out of this talk concerning the human-like actions of certain animals, grew, naturally, references to the animals that appear with human attributes in the many fireside tales so dear to the hearts of the people.

Sobah was recognized as the story-teller of the village, and so when mention was made of the deer that coughed, Oleemah proposed that Sobah should tell them the story of how the deer acquired such a habit, adding diplomatically, "Yo' pass we all fo' pull story good fashion."

The story-teller was already in a gracious frame of mind, and, pleased with this last tribute to his art, lost no time in responding with a legend of Creation's early dawn.

## Goro, The Wonderful Wrestler.

"One tem all dem beef (animals) dey gadder to one place, all dem beef dis wuld, but de head of dem all, dat now one ooman en he pickin (pickaninny). De pickin name Goro. One net big rain fa' down, he out all de fiah. Now de mawnin' cole, all dem beef dey trimble, dey cole too much. No fiah no deh fo' make demse'f wa'm. Dey see one leelee place deh wey smoke duh come out. Dey sen' Deer, dem say:

"'Go bring fiah fo' we, over yandah to dat place.'

"Deer go, he meet de ooman en he pickin wey duh sit down close de fiah. Dey try wa'm demse'f by de fiah. W'en Deer reach he tell de ooman 'Mawnin'; he say: "I come beg fiah."

"De ooman say, 'I nebber greedy (begrudge) pusson fiah, but I get one law heah. Pusson wey wan' fiah mus' fet (fight) wid me pickin, mus' beat um. Yo' see de leelee girl? One place outside dah do', he nar (is) de fet place, he rub, he smooth. Go fet me pickin; ef yo' beat um yo' take de fiah.'

"De Deer he look de pickin foolish nah heen[7] yi, he say:

"'Mammy, yo' wan' make I kill yo' pickin?'

"De ooman say: 'Nebber min', kill um, de fault not yo' yown.'

"Deer say: 'All ret.'

"De pickin come, dey two grip, dey begin fo' fet, de ooman begin fo' sing; he duh sing fo' he pickin, he no duh sing fo' de Deer. He sing:

> "'Goro, Goro,
> Fet like how yo' bin fet ebery day,
> Tay (until) all de groun' duh shake.'"

As if in sympathy with the rhythm of the song, Sobah's whole body began to sway back and forth, his voice rose and fell in musical cadences, and his hands began to clap in time to the movement of the song. All the listeners took up the rhythmic swaying of the body and the measured clapping of the hands, and as soon as they caught the words, joined heartily in the chant. Not satisfied with the first result, Sobah led off with a repetition. This time there was no occasion for dissatisfaction, and the story proceeded with increasing animation.

The Deer after fighting with Goro.

"Goro fet, he fet. He hase (raised) de Deer up; de Deer go take one yeah up befo' he come down. W'en he fa' down he get cough. Some tem ef yo' deh nah (in) bush en Deer cough, yo' go say, 'Nar (is) pusson.'"

"Dat nar true," broke in Dogbah eagerly, a spark of understanding falling on his dull mind. "Mese'f bin hearee um cough to-day nah bush. Dah fa' wey he bin fa' long tem make he cough so," and he shook with laughter, as if Mr. Deer's hard fall were highly amusing.

Sobah, taking up the interrupted thread of the narrative, said: "Well, Deer go home widout no fiah."

"Elephan' he say: 'I go go, I jus' wrap me mout' 'pon dis girl I twis' um, I hase (raise) um up, I wop um down, I take de fiah.' Well he begin root dem big, big 'tick wid he teet' fo' show how he 'trong; he say: 'Nar *so* I go meet de girl.'

"Well, w'en Elephan' go, he tell de ooman how do, he meet de fiah, he wan' take um. De ooman say: 'All ret,' he say: 'Look me pickin. Go fet.' De pickin begin, de ooman sing de same sing w'en dey grip fo' fet.

"'Goro, Goro,
Fet lek how yo' bin fet ebery day,
Tay all de groun' duh shake.'"

This time the apt imitators caught up the refrain at once, and gave it with great zest. "Soon," continued Sobah, after a momentary pause, "de girl he hase de Elephan' up, he sen' um up; but since de Elephan' stout he no able, he jus' sen' um up as far as one week. De one week finish, de Elephan' come down. W'en he fa' down 'pon de groun' he hurt he teet', en he teet' swell. Dat make Elephan' he teeth big."

At this point Sobah struck an attitude suggestive of the Elephant's state of general dilapidation. His face took on a look of mingled pain and disgust, and this in turn was succeeded by a smile of self-approbation, and ended in a peculiar chuckling laugh that carried infectious mirth to all the circle of listeners.

The Elephant after the fight with the Goro.

Settling back once more to his usual air of serious dignity, Sobah continued his recital.

"Elephan' he go back, he no kare any fiah.

"Well, Lepped come, he tell de ooman say: 'I come fo' fiah.'

"De ooman say, 'All ret,' he say, 'Look me pickin, he go fet yo.'

"Dey begin fo' fet, Goro en Lepped. Dey fet en fet. De girl he hase (raise) de Lepped up; he sen' um, he go, he take t'ree mont'; he come down, he fa' down 'pon 'tone, he cut hese'f, de blood sprinkle all 'pon um. Dat make de Lepped he spot, spot."

This explanation of the Leopard's spots, seemed reasonable enough to these simple-minded people, who ask only that some cause out of the ordinary should account for ordinary things. Dogbah was about to offer a comment again, but before his slow wits could formulate his words, the story-teller had plunged into the next sentence.

"De Lepped he go widout no fiah. De beef, w'en dey see um, dey say:

"'Eh! We no get no fiah to-day.'

"Now Puss he get up, he say: 'I go go.'

"Dem beef dey laugh um, dey say: 'All ret.' Dey say: 'Yo' see all dem big beef? Dey go, dey no able fo' bring fiah. Yo' say yo' duh go? All ret, go try.'

"De Cat he go, he say: 'Mammy, I come fo' fiah.'

"De ooman say: 'All ret, go try wid me pickin.'

"De Cat go, de ooman begin fo' sing. De girl he jus' take de Cat wid one han', he hebe (raise) um up, he go take one yeah en ha'f befo' he come down. He fa' hard, he begin fo' cry 'Meouw! meouw!' Dat make Puss duh cry anytem, net or day tem he duh cry. He go home widout no fiah.

"Now Spider go, he say, 'Mammy, I come fo' fiah.'

"De ooman say: 'All ret, oonah (you) go fet wid me pickin.' De ooman he no even se'f sing. Dah girl take Spider wid one fingah, he hebe (raise) um up fo' two yeah."

A murmur of dissent caused the story-teller to pause and cast a look of inquiry around the company. It was evident that the ardent admirers of crafty little Mr. Spider could not bear to have him disposed of so easily. But Sobah checked the rising protest by a commanding gesture, and a look that seemed to say: "I am sorry, but I must tell the story just as it is." When the silence assured him of a hearing, he continued.

"W'en Spider come he fa' down, he broke he foot. Dat make

Spider duh crawl now; dat make he walker wid four foot, sometem six. Long tem[8] he walker wid two foot 'traight lek pusson. Spider go home widout no fiah.

"Cunnie Rabbit he go, he say: 'Mammy, I come fo' fiah.'

"De ooman say: 'All ret, go to dah pickin, fet wid um.'

"W'en dey fet, de girl come hebe (raise) um up, he take six mont.' De t'ing wey make he no go far, he get too much sense."

This was uttered with peculiar emphasis, and was answered by a prolonged "Y-a-h-oh; y-a-h-oh!" of assent that indicated a keen appreciation of Cunnie Rabbit's superior mental qualities. The next sentence was almost equally satisfactory, and regained for the story what favor it had lost by the humiliation of Mr. Spider.

"W'en Cunnie Rabbit come down he fa' down, he get up one tem (at once), he begin fo' run, he *run*. Dat make tay (until) to-day he hard fo' ketch. He kin run fas' pass all dem beef.

"All de odder beef duh go, dey no able fo' beat de pickin. Conk (snail) he get up, he go, he walker 'bout slow, slow. W'en he tell dem beef: 'I go go fo' fiah,' Cunnie Rabbit take um en hebe (threw) um nah (out) de do'. He fa' down, he hurt hese'f, he get blood 'pon um. De blood mark, mark um, but he say: 'Nebber min', I go go.'

De Conk.

"He go, he tell de ooman, 'How do;' he say, 'Mammy I come fo' fiah, en I mus' kare dis fiah go home.'

"De ooman say: 'All ret; look de place wey fo' fet wid me pickin.

"De Conk do lek he duh walk 'roun de place slow, slow; but he duh get slipple (slippery) spit, he duh rub all de place. W'en he done finis' fo' rub, he say: 'Come fet now.'

"De girl come, he duh boas', he no know de cunnie wey de Conk bin pull fo' beat um. Den grip fo' fet, he en de Conk. De Conk he hase (raise) de girl up, he go fo' five yeah. De ooman no see he pickin, he duh cry. Conk take de fiah, he go home. Dey cook, dey yeat, dey gladee. Dey done finis' fo' cook en yeat befo' de girl fa' down. W'en de ooman see how de Conk hebe (raise) he pickin up, he begin fo' cry. Nar (It is) de ooman bring cry nah (into) de wuld.

"Story come, story go."

This well-known form of ending was followed by a long silence. The night was already far advanced, but the black man is a creature of the night. Deeper than the color of his skin lies his kinship with the darkness, however much he may dread the powers of evil that creep forth as soon as the day is gone.

At last the silence was broken by Gondomah, a man of modest bearing, who, though seldom essaying the rôle of a story-teller, could not yet be reconciled to the place assigned to Spider in the last story. Half to himself he said: "Spider nar smart man, nobody no go pass um." Then, emboldened by the sound of his own voice, and by the encouraging silence, he proceeded in the fewest possible words to relate how.

## Mr. Spider Sold A Very Fine Dog.

"One tem Spider say he go go far up country fo' buy plenty cow. Early mawnin', fus' fowl crow, he grap (got up), he walker tay (until) de sun middle de sky. He done tire. W'en he reach to one big, *big* grass-fiel' he go lay down. He close to one lion, but he no know. Dey all two, dey duh sleep. Well, soon de Foulah people dey bring plenty cow wey dem duh kare down fo' go sell. De Foulah people dey no sabbee lion, dey nebber see um yet. W'en dey meet dis lion heah de one man say:

"'Eh, lookee! Wey t'ing dat?'

"Odder one say: 'He big dog, aintee?'

"Den 'tan' up wid wonder. Dey no see Spider fo' long tem, because he leelee so. W'en dey fus' meet up nah grass-fiel' Spider bin hearee um, he come out heen sleep. He hearee how dey say dat de lion one big dog. W'en he look de plenty cow he t'ink: 'How I go do fo' get dem cow? I mus' get um.'

"He grap (got up), he tell dem Foulah man 'How do.' Dey answer um 'tankee.' Dey ax um say:

"'Daddy, now dis dog heah, yo' get um?'

Mr. Spider sells a very fine dog.

"Spider say: 'Yes, nar me yown dog dat.'

"De Foulah man wan' fo' buy um, dey talk de palaver, dey bargain fo' gie um all de cow fo' buy dis dog. Spider say: 'All ret, but no wake dis dog yeah, oh! because he done use me too much.[9] Bimeby w'en yo' wake um, he go follow me, he no 'gree fo' follow oonah (you). W'en I done go far 'way, den oonah mus' wake um.'"

By this time Gondomah was warming to his theme, and surprised even himself with his unwonted eloquence. The listeners, ever ready to see a rich point, had for some time been quivering with intense appreciation of Spider's rascally shrewdness, and just here gave expression to their delight in a fit of uncontrollable laughter, and exclamations of approval.

Gondomah, elated beyond measure, paused long enough to regain his composure, and then went on.

"So den people dey gie Spider all de cow. Dey wait tay (until) he done get far 'way, dey begin fo' call de dog. Jus' de Lion wake he open he yi, he 'tretch hese'f, he raise he tail, take um put um 'pon he back. He jus' grip one of de Foulah people, he kill um; de odder all run go. Spider he done get de cow.

"So ef Spider tell yo' say he go do anyt'ing, no deny.[10]

Sobah, a little jealous of the attention that had been paid to this upstart story-teller, had been searching in the vast storehouse of his memory for a fitting tale with which to bring himself again into favorable notice. The one which came to his mind caused a broad smile to spread over his face, and a chuckle of satisfaction to rise in his throat. Oleemah, noticing these signs of pleasure, and suspecting that they foreshadowed a good story, asked encouragingly:

"Wey t'ing make yo' gladee so? Do, yah? tell we."

Not needing further urging, Sobah launched into his narrative with much animation.

## Mr. Turtle Makes A Riding-Horse Of Mr. Leopard.

"One day Trorkey (Turtle) bin walker close to Lepped he ho'se (house), en he see de ooman lepped 'tan' up nah de do'-(door) mout'. He tell um say:

"'How do, Mammy? How yo' kin 'tan'?'

"De Mammy answer um: 'Tankee, I well leelee bit, how yo'se'f, Daddy? I no bin see yo' long tem.'

"Trorkey answer um: 'I no so well, Mammy; dis de hour w'en feber duh walker all 'bout, en me skin all duh hurt. I duh go to de bush fo' pull med'cin', fo' make leelee tea. Which side Mr. Lepped to-day?'

"He wef answer: 'He done go walker; I duh wait um jus' now. Yo' no bin see um nah road?'

"Trorkey say: 'No, I no bin see um. I sorry he done go, because ef he here I go ride um lek hoss.'

"Lepped he wef deny, he say:

"'No, yo' won' do um, yo' no go able ride me man lek hoss.'

"Den Trorkey go home. W'en Lepped come nah ho'se he wef tell um say:

"'Trorkey bin pass heah to-day, he say he go ride yo' lek hoss.'

"Well, den de man lepped vex, he run go to Trorkey, he go ax um ef he bin say he go ride um lek hoss. Trorkey deny, he say:

"'I no say so.'

"Den Lepped say: 'All ret. Come, we go ax me wef.'

"Den de Trorkey say: 'I no able fo' walk. De sick too 'trong 'pon me.'

"Dat de cunnie he duh do.

"De Lepped say: 'Come, I go tote yo', I go ax me wef.'

"Den de Trorkey say: 'Gie me one leelee rope, make I tie um 'roun yo' mout', make I hole um, so w'en I duh shake, shake, make I no fa' down.'

"En de Lepped gie um de rope.

"Well, de Trorkey say: 'Gie me one leelee 'tick, make I go flog dem fly, make I go dribe dem w'en dey duh follow we.'

This bit of apparently artless guile on the part of Mr. Turtle, threatened to convulse the audience, but interest in the development of the story had become so intense as to check the rising tide of mirth for the present, while the story-teller went on with growing enthusiasm.

"Well, de Lepped gie um de 'tick.'

"Den Trorkey he say, 'Come go now.'

"Well, w'en de Lepped done kare Trorkey go, Trorkey duh joomp, he duh flog de Lepped, he duh make lek pusson wey duh ride hoss.'

Mr. Turtle makes a riding-horse of Mr. Leopard.

Sobah described this little episode with inimitable drollery in tone and manner, and ended the 'wey duh ride hoss', with a peculiar nasal explosion that served to emphasize the humor of the situation. The result was instantaneous, and convulsive laughter continued many minutes, breaking out afresh every time anyone would remark: 'Aintee he flog um good fashion?' When the laughter had subsided sufficiently, the story proceeded:

"W'en dey go meet Lepped he wef nah road, de ooman laugh en say:

"'Oh! Nar true wey dis Trorkey bin talk, say he go ride me man lek hoss, so nar true.'

"W'en Lepped reach, he hebe Trorkey down, den he tell he wef, he say:

"I done bring Trorkey come, fo' de word he duh talk, say he go ride me lek hoss.'

"He wef say: 'Wey t'ing Trorkey do so? He no ride yo' lek hoss'? en de ooman laugh agin.

"Now Lepped see Trorkey bin make he fool; he ketch Trorkey, he tie um 'pon one big 'tick, he flog um sotay (until) he back all cut, cut. Dat make sotay to-day de mark all lef 'pon Trorkey he back."

There was more laughter at the retribution that overtook Mr. Turtle, and then the talk drifted to personal matters.

Finally, as if led by some common impulse, the company began to disperse, some to the solid comfort of a hard mud bed, and some to consort with the hideous spirits of darkness and the night.

## CHAPTER III

# A BACK-YARD KITCHEN

SOBAH had gone with his boat on a trading trip to Freetown, but he was a thoughtful husband and father, and had left a generous supply of rice and dried fish.

Mammy Mamenah and Konah were leisurely preparing their evening meal, for once alone. No, not entirely alone, for in their kitchen, which was also the back-yard, was gathered just at this time a strangely assorted group of creatures more or less intimately connected with the household. By mutual consent, some precedence of rights seemed to be granted to the two human beings, but they did not seem to be inclined to exercise their rights to any oppressive degree. In dress and bearing they were almost as simple and blissfully unconscious as the other creatures that shared their back-yard space with them. Konah's sole attire was a string of beads fastened around her waist, while Mammy Mamenah had the conventional piece of cloth, three feet wide, wrapped around her body, tucked deftly beneath her arms, and extending to her knees. Chickens roamed over the place with the air of rightful ownership. Goats nibbled the bits of grass that grew around the edge of the bare spot, and climbed over or peered into anything that appealed to their curiosity. A monkey, limited in his activities by the length of string fastened around his slender body, was going through various evolutions in the endeavor to reach the tail feathers of a parrot that was shrilly scolding at a mangy little dog. The furnishings of the kitchen were few and simple in the extreme. The stove consisted of three stones so arranged as to support a pot of rice, and at the same time to allow a fire to be kindled beneath. A large pot for the rice, a smaller one for the stew, some calabashes and a large mortar and pestle for pounding the rice, completed the outfit. The rice had been set to boil, and Mammy Mamenah had nothing to do but wait for it to cook. She had seated herself upon one end of a small log, the other end of which was in the fire. Konah had squatted upon the ground in front of her mother, and by artful and suggestive questions was endeavoring to draw out a story about some of her animal friends. A heathen mother does not concern herself about the pleasure of her child, and takes no trouble for the child's happiness, unless there is some amusement in it for herself, but Konah was the third child, the two older ones having died of small-pox, and on that account was treated more nearly with indulgence than were other children. A spirit of comradeship, almost of affection, had grown up between this black mother and her story-loving child. The many hours they had passed together had tended to deepen the feeling of fellowship and sympathy.

Finally Konah put her desire in the form of a direct entreaty, 'Mammy, do yah (please) pull story.'

In response Mammy Mamenah drew the child's head down upon her lap, and, loosening the kinky wool, proceeded to replait it in innumerable little braids that caused the jet-black hair on the shapely head to stand out in regular rows like the ridges of a cantaloupe.

"'Yo' lek story too much,' she said reprovingly; then, repenting almost immediately, added: 'Wey t'ing yo' wan'?'

The question was unnecessary, for the child's very pronounced preference for Cunning Rabbit, above all the creatures of her fairy world, was well known to her mother. So in a low crooning voice she began the story of

## Cunning Rabbit And His Well.

"Long tem, Cunnie Rabbit en all dem beef bin gadder. Den meet up to one place fo' talk palaver, because de country dry too much. Dey no get one grain (drop) wattah sotay (until) all man wan' fo' die. Dey all get word fo' talk, f'om de big beef to de small, but nobody no able fo' fine sense fo' pull dem f'om dis yeah big trouble. Cunnie Rabbit he no bin say notting, he jus' listen wey dem beef talk; he t'ink say: 'Wey ting I go do fo' get wattah?'

"Bimeby he grap (get up), he go home, he begin fo' dig well. He dig, he dig, he *dig*. De wattah come plenty. He drink sotay (until) he done satisfy.

Cunning Rabbit and his well.

"Now dem beef hearee dat Cunnie Rabbit get well. Spider he grap fo' go walker to Cunnie Rabbit. He say:

"'Fren', we no get one grain wattah fo' drink, we go die. Make yo' gie we.

"Cunnie Rabbit tell um, he say:

"'De pusson wey wan' make me gie um wattah, make he come fet me.'

"Spider say: 'All ret.'

"Now Spider en Cunnie Rabbit dey fet. Cunnie Rabbit hase (raise) Spider up to dah sky. He come down, he lay down flat. He grap (get up), he hase Cunnie Rabbit up. Cunnie Rabbit go to de sky; he blow one horn wey (which) he hole nah (in) he han'. W'en he blow um dark come, w'en he blow um agin, do' clean.[11] He fa' down, he grip de wuld, VIP! He han' long, dey go inside de groun'. Cunnie Rabbit get up back, he hase Spider up. One rainy season, one dry season he stay 'pon top de sky. W'en he come down, w'en he too fa' down 'pon de groun', he say: 'Ee! Ee! Ee! Fren', I no able agin. Den he shake Cunnie Rabbit he han'; he say: 'Oonah (you) 'trong man.'"

To the recital of this very extraordinary combat between two very unusual people, Konah had been listening so intently that her restless limbs forgot to move, and her breathing was partly suspended. A movement of relief at this point in the narrative, and a long sigh of satisfaction at the sensible outcome of the contest, showed that her sympathy with the characters of the story was warm and real. She shifted her position, stooped to pull a chigger from one of her little black toes, then curled her head down on the other side for the comfortable enjoyment of the tale, which was continued while the tiny braids took form under the mother's deft fingers. The resumption of the story was delayed just a little; for two children, Konah's playmates, catching the echo of a story through the open door of the hut, came to share the pleasure. Mamenah, finding more amusement in entertaining a larger audience, proceeded with greater energy.

"Dem beef all come, dey try, dey no able. Elephan' come, he say:

"'Wey de man wey say he de mos' 'trong? Make he come one tem, make we fet, so I go take wattah. I too t'irst.'

"Cunnie Rabbit come, he boas', he say: 'Nar (it is) *me* dis.'

"Elephan' take he long mout', he wrap Cunnie Rabbit, he wrap um 'trong. He fling um, turn, turn um, he hebe um up, so he jam to de sky. De sweat wey he bin sweat, dat nar de hair 'pon heen skin. Cunnie Rabbit come, he 'tan' up, he hase de Elephan' up."

"Cunnie Rabbit wey leelee so," chuckled Konah, unable to restrain her satisfaction at the prowess of her hero, but the interruption was unnoted.

"Elephan' heen long mout' come nah groun', he wrap den 'tick fo' hole hese'f, he broke um w'en he go up. He say: 'Cunnie Rabbit wey leelee so, nar *he* do me so?'

"He hole Cunnie Rabbit wid heen long mout' agin, he drag um, he make big noise 'pon de groun' w'en he drag um. He pin Cunnie Rabbit down; den (they) fet, den fet, den fet. De place wey den fet he big pass (bigger than) dis town, he double um four tem fo' big. Dey fet tay (till) fiah ketch dah place. Dah one wey box he cumpin, fiah ketch; dah odder one wey box he cumpin, fiah ketch. De place he bu'n clean, so-so san'-san' (sand) lef' no mo'."[12]

Here the narrator's voice, momentarily pitched to a higher key, exclaimed: "Make yo' dribe dem goat, dey do rascal trick;" and the child, only less nimble than the goats, drove with an 'Ah! hey!' an inquisitive one from dangerous proximity to the greens, made ready to be put into the stew. The animal retreated to a short distance, with an air that indicated contemplated return at the first opportunity, while Konah turned a calabash over the greens, pushed the log further into the fire, and sat down to pick into bits the dried fish, so that her mother might be left to do uninterrupted justice to the marvellous contest of "dem beef."

"Well, dem beef dey all duh try, dey no know how fo' do. Dey all go make bargain. All dem beef dey pull (bring) plenty clo'es, so plenty dey done full dis town heah, dey full Freetown. En dis yeah clo'es dey gie um all to Cunnie Rabbit. Dey say: '*Do*;[13] ef yo' no gie we wattah we go die.'

"Cunnie Rabbit say: 'All ret. Make all man take one one cup wattah drink.'

"But de bargain *dis*. Ef de pusson no done *all*, he fo' take one piece clot' en gie um to Cunnie Rabbit, en say: 'Dis nar fo' de wattah weh I wais.' De cup he cover dis whole town, he cover 'Merica, he cover Englan', he cover Freetown fo' big oh!"[14]

The sparkling eyes and white teeth of the little listeners indicated their appreciation of this enormous conception, but they were too eager for the story to interrupt.

"Now Elephan' say: 'Make me fus' drink.'

"He take de cup, he full um nah well. He put heen long mout inside so, he draw de wattah; he draw um, he draw um, he draw um sotay he done um. Lepped say: 'Make me come try.' Dey full de cup, Lepped he drink, he drink, he *drink* sotay (until) he done de wattah. De beef all drink, dey all done um. Den leelee beef dey done de wattah inside de big cup. Dey all no able fo' go agin. Fo' walker go home dem no able, but den able fo' grap (get up to) cook. Dey cook big, big, *big* ress (rice). De pot fo' cook de ress—Lie man say de pot big lek dis whole town heah, Grimah all, Moshengo all. Well, me wey no duh lie, I no lie *anyt'ing*, I jus' put leelee salt fo' make he sweet, I say he big lek all Temne country, all white man country, double all two, I put half 'pon um agin en mo' town, so de pot big."

This climax elicited from Konah an explosive little exclamation. She cracked together the tips of her fingers, rolled over on the ground, then righting herself, asked:

"Mammy, how yo' t'ink say dey go able done dah *big* ress?"

Very contemptuous, very subduing was the voice in reply:

"Aintee yo' know say long tem (long time ago) dem beef able anyt'ing?" Then resuming the crooning tone: "Dey yeat dah ress, goat all, cow all, fowl, sheep, all dem elephan', dey yeat dah ress.

"One big, big wattah spread 'pon dem all, dey all no know which side he come out. De ashes f'om de fiah he spread 'pon dem beef all. Well, dey all swim, dey all go to dem yown home. One tem beef all bin white, but since w'en de ashes bin deh 'pon dem long tem, some kin (can be) red, some kin brown, some black, some spot-spot."

Mammy Mamenah's tale was told, and she turned now to her fish and greens, her pepper, palm-oil and pea-nuts, to prove herself as able to make a palatable stew for the rice now cooked, as she was to tell a story.

As these articles were being placed in the pot, the children looked on with swelling anticipations of a feast sufficient to satisfy the most extravagant demands of their keen appetites, as of course the openhearted hospitality characteristic of the country, would keep the little visitors to share the rice and stew.

"Make yo' put plenty peppy, Mammy," urged Konah, with an eagerness that betrayed her weakness for that fiery condiment.

"Shut mout'", replied the woman, with much more gruffness than she felt, but nevertheless she put in a generous supply of the little red fire-balls.

Soon the stew was over the fire, and once more they all sat

down to wait. Konah, with her dreamy mind full of the story she had just heard, and her eyes full of the new light of dawning intelligence, sat watching the goats that were frisking and playing about the yard. It began to break in dimly upon her mind that all those antics might have meaning apart from the present, and might spring from some dim remembrance of experiences from the long ago, when the animals belonged to a higher order of beings.

Just then one of the goats dropped to its knees and began to rub its neck along the grass.

"Ah, Mammy!" exclaimed the little girl excitedly, "yo' see dah goat? W'ey t'ing dat he do?"

"He 'member how he bin swim, long tem," answered the woman somewhat indifferently. "Not to kratch he duh kratch,[15] but to swim he duh swim long tem, w'en de ocean come 'pon de beef all."

Another goat, some distance away, was chewing its cud with much energy and determination. The process attracted the children, one of whom raised a question as to its meaning.

"Yo' no know dat?" replied Mamenah, this time with growing interest. "Dat nar de ress wey dey yeat long tem. He no done yet; goat, cow, dey duh yeat all tem, even net tem, day tem, dey yeat dah ress."

A frisky kid was playfully kicking up its heels, and anon leaping into the air.

"Wey t'ing make he do dat?" asked Konah, laughing gleefully at the antics of the kid.

The woman, now thoroughly in sympathy with the children's questions, launched into a series of explanations without waiting for further inquiries.

"W'en de goat bin come out de wattah wid swim, so he bin dry hese'f, he bin wipe de wattah f'om he skin, he bin kick en kick. Lookee! Yo' see dah goat wey duh 'tan' up yandah, duh shake heen yase (ears) so? Dat de cole wey bin 'pon um long tem, duh make he yase trimble tay now."

"Eh! hey! Yo' see how dah goat duh lay down *so*, heen head 'pon 'tick? *So* he bin do fo' blow (breathe) w'en he done tire fo' swim."

"Ah! I duh watch dem. Hey! Yo' see dem turn dem tail so?"

The goat was wriggling its tail so that it looked not unlike a paddle in rapid motion. "Dat nar paddle wey duh he'p um fo' pull; he bin turn um fas' fas' w'en he inside de wattah."

Two goats were standing on their hind legs, playing, and two others were engaged in a mock fight. These manœuvres needed explanation, and Mammy Manenah went on after a momentary pause. "W'en de goat wan' tell Cunnie Rabbit 'How do,' dah tem w'en he go beg wattah, *so* he bin 'tan' up fus' tem. W'en dey fet dey 'member say how dey fet long tem wid Cunnie Rabbit. Dat make dem try agin."

By this time two of the animals were solemnly touching noses, and seemed to be discussing some grave matter. To an inquiry of the children as to the meaning of this behavior, the reply came: "Oh dat? Nar bargain dem make long tem fo' get wattah."

A plaintive little bleat brought out the explanation: "Long tem, w'en one leelee goat bin go beg de wattah, Cunnie Rabbit say: 'Make yo' call yo' Mammy, make he come;' den de pickin say: 'Mah! mah!' Dat make de leelee goat say 'Mah mah,' tay (till) to-day."

Then reminded of another characteristic goat trait, she continued earnestly:

"Aintee yo' see w'en one goat kin run, all start wid run fo' follow um? Cunnie Rabbit bin sen' one say: 'Make dem call all, make dem come drink wattah f'om dah big cup.' Now 'member dey duh 'member.

"Dey gladee w'en pusson call um fo' yeat, dey run. Dey 'member w'en Cunnie Rabbit say: 'Who no come fo' yeat dah ress, he go meet um done."

A goat that had been making a tour of inspection around the yard, was just now peering inquisitively over the edge of a large barrel, an unusual acquisition from Sobah's last trading trip to Freetown.

"Oh dah goat deh?" This in reply to a look of inquiry from the children. "Long tem he go peep inside well, w'en he no get one grain wattah. He duh peep inside Cunnie Rabbit heen well."

"Goat no 'fraid pusson?"—this after an interval of silence—"Oh! Yo know fo' wey t'ing dey no go 'fraid pusson? I tell yo' 'bout um. Spider make dem lek pusson," and with that she drifted off naturally into an account of Mr. Spider and the goats, and incidentally showed why some goats are tame, and others wild.

## Goats Of The Wood And Of The Town.

"Spider he bin pusson, long tem, he no bin 'tan' lek[16] to-day; he done turn odder kine of t'ing now. Dah tem he get big, big, big cassada (cassava) fa'm. He say: Make dem goat all come tell um 'How do.' Den he go root cassada, he root cassada; he pile um high, he jam de sky fo' high. He tell dem goat, he say: 'Who wan' go nah town, make he go nah town; who wan' go nah bush, make he go nah bush. Now he shabe (divided) de cassada. All dem wey say dey wan' go nah town, he gie um four, four stick cassada;[17] he say: 'Aintee me pusson? Yo' mus' lek pusson.'

"Dey say: 'All ret.'

"De one wey (who) wan' go nah bush, he gie dem two, two 'tick. Dat make sotay (till) now, dem bush-goat no lek pusson, dey say dey wan' be inside bush."

A cow that had been grazing just behind the fence, came up now and looked over into the yard, at the same time switching her tail in a vigorous attempt to dislodge a large fly that had settled upon her back. Konah noticed this interesting performance, and glad of the opportunity to seek further explanations, aroused her mother from the reverie into which she had fallen, with the question:

"Yo' see de cow wey 'tan' up yandah? Wey t'ing do he bin make heen tail so, knock um behine heen back?"

The efforts of the cow now became almost frantic, much to the delight of the children. Mamenah explained:

"W'en dey bin swim, long tem, he tie one big, big cassada to heen tail fo' cham (chew). Wen he wan' fo' cham um, he turn um, knock um 'pon heen back, so he kin turn cham um. So yo' kin see cow 'tan' up, knock heen tail behine back. Not to fly he duh dribe, dat cassada he bin 'member, long tem."

After this last explanation, there was silence for some minutes, until the children, returning from the land of dreams to that of reality, became aware that they were exceedingly hungry. The rice had sometime since been removed from the fire and beneath its grass-woven cover had steamed until now the stew was ready to pour over it. Konah ran to the brook, and returned with a calabash of water, and the little company crouched upon the ground to enjoy what to them was a succulent repast. Balls of rice of considerable size were squeezed up, and by a deft motion of the hand were transferred to the mouth, until the appetites were thoroughly appeased. Finally even Konah cared for nought else but to throw herself listlessly back against a tree that stood near, and, lolling out her tongue, she fanned it with a shred from a banana leaf to quench the fire of the coveted cayenne. It was hot, nevertheless the torture was delicious. Sweet, very sweet is "peppy" to an African palate, and how much is enough is a problem dependent largely upon the supply.

CHAPTER IV

# EVENING ON THE WATER

SOBAH was a born trader, in this respect exemplifying one of the strongest propensities of his tribe. He had frequently made trading trips "up country," and had sometimes taken a boat-load of produce even to the markets of Freetown. To-day the spirit of commerce possessed him again. Securing a crew of six to man his boat, he passed the day in collecting his stores and stowing them away on board. Hampers of rice, palm-oil, pepper, kola-nuts, country cloths, rubber and ivory, the latter secured in barter from an "up country" chief, comprised the cargo. A white fowl was placed in the bow of the boat, in the belief that its presence would ensure a prosperous voyage.

Late in the afternoon, as the full tide was about to ebb, the boat pushed out into the current, and the six sturdy boatmen settled themselves for an all-night row to the mouth of the river. Soon their oars were swinging in perfect time, and the weird melody of the native boating-song seemed to bind boat, tide, swaying bodies and plying oars into one inseparable harmony of sound and motion.

If the souls of these children of Nature had been as responsive to sights of beauty and loveliness as they were to rhythmical motion and sound, they would have thrilled with admiration and delight at the panorama brought to view by a sudden turn in the river. Great mangrove trees, leaning over to whisper to their neighbors on the other shore, intertwined their huge branches in a lofty archway over the stream. Thickets of shrubbery filled all the intervening spaces, and tumbled over the river bank. Tropical vines, wild, entangled, luxuriant, trailed over all and hung in graceful festoons of green from the branches of the trees. Banked along the water's edge were masses of calla-like lilies, interspersed with ferns. Out of the mass of verdure on the river bank, peeped the bright crimson leaves that, crowning the ends of the branches, served as flowers on a shrub whose other foliage was of the deepest green. Near by another shrub displayed a whorl of leaves like unto the foliage in shape and form, but creamy white, arranged around the tiniest suggestion of a flower. Birds of bright plumage flitted here and there among the trees, monkeys chattered and scolded in the leafy depths, and snakes suspended their sinuous bodies from tall canes, or were coiled upon beds of moss. Alligators lay basking lazily in the evening sun.

Looking down the river from the bend, the stream seemed to be one continuous avenue of green, with occasional touches of color. Save for the sinister suggestion from the presence of the snakes and the alligators, the spot might have been a bit of fairy-land so quiet and so isolated that it seemed no human being had ever invaded its sanctity. It was a place to cause the cultured heart to go out in reverence to meet the spirit of the Infinite.

But our scantily clad boatmen had no eye for all this beauty, no soul to vibrate in unison with the sacred scene. On the other hand, their hearts were filled with dread and superstitious fears.

To their beclouded minds the place seemed haunted by unseen spirits of evil. An alligator slipped with a little splash into the water and disappeared from sight. The sun now sinking in the west, cast ominous shadows amid the thickening foliage. The hearts of the boatmen were filled with a nameless dread, their song died entirely away, and, dropping a piece of silver into the water to propitiate the spirit of the river, they raised their oars lest the sound of rowing should disturb the genius of the place, and floated with the tide in almost breathless silence until the boat reached the broader waters beyond. Then breathing more freely, they began to row again, gently at first, but with gradually increased speed until the oars were in full swing to the echo of the boating-song.

The first streaks of day found them at the bar-mouth, but a strong gale from the sea made it impossible to proceed, and they were compelled to anchor for an indefinite period. Tired out with the night's rowing, the men doubled up in positions of varying discomfort, and slept soundly for many hours. Aroused at last, they kindled a fire in the box of gravel in the bow of the boat, cooked a bountiful supply of rice and fish, and, gathering around the great rice-pot, they proceeded to stow away the food in such quantities as only a black man's stomach can contain.

All through the remainder of the day the gale continued with but slight abatement. It was plain that the night also must be spent at anchor before the voyage could be resumed. The evening meal was a repetition of that of the morning, quantity not excepted, and after it was over they entertained themselves in their own peculiar way. Full stomachs brought on an amiable frame of mind, and the gathering shades of evening developed a feeling of sociability and loosened the tongues of the men. The hour was auspicious for story-telling. The physical man was at ease, there was time and to spare, and the gathering night drove the mind in upon itself.

Under such circumstances stories were inevitable, and needed only some suggestion to set them going. Dogbah's capacity for rice, shown a little before at their evening meal, was the occasion of a rather coarse jest, at which all the men, including the victim, laughed heartily.

That reminded Sobah of the same propensity in Mr. Spider, the impersonation of most of the black man's virtues, and many of his vices. With a merry twinkle in his eye, and a suggestive shrug of his shoulders, Sobah shifted to a more commanding position, preparatory to beginning his story.

The men, accustomed to receive half their communications through signs more or less occult, understood at once what was coming, and put themselves into listening attitudes. The story was full of life and movement, and was entered into with much spirit by both narrator and listeners.

## Spider Discovers The Wax Girl.

"Spider bin get fa'm wey (where) be bin lib wid heen wef en heen pickin (pickaninnies). Dis yeah fa'm bin big, oh! en de ress plenty, but wey (since) Spider nebber satisfy fo' yeat, he greedy (begrudged) heen wef en heen pickin all. He make one plan fo' heself fo' make dem lef he one (alone) nah fa'm.[18]

"He tell he wef, say: 'Dah tem w'en I go die, yo' mus' bury me close me fa'm-ho'se.'

Mr. Spider pretends to die.

"Aftah he done tell heen wef dat, he no' tay agin,[19] Spider he bin sick, he head duh hurt um fo' true, true. He no able fo' yeat anyt'ing agin. He say dah sick 'trong 'pon um. Jus' t'ree no mo (merely), well, Spider he die. He wef en heen pickin' dey cry fo' um, en dem people all. Dey bury um close de fa'm-ho'se lek how he bin say. Well, net tem he wef take all he pickin, he go nah town, but sun tem dey wuk nah fa'm. W'en dey wan' fo' go back nah town, dey bin lef clean ress plenty, den bin lef fis' en palm-ile, en peppy, en all t'ing fo' cook.

"W'en dey done go, Spider get up soffle f'om he grabe, he go inside fa'm-ho'se, he go take pot, he was' um, he put um nah fiah, he cook plenty ress; he go look, he take fis', he take 'nuff fo' hese'f. Well, he kin yeat dat all net sotay fus' fowl crow. Jus' w'en fowl crow, Spider go back nah he grabe. He go lay down deh soffle. Dem people dey come now. W'en dey wan' cook dey go look den ress, dey meet only leelee bit. Dem no know who take um. Well,

Spider do dis trick ebery net fo' one week. W'en den people go home, Spider bin come out f'om he grabe. Dem people heah dey no know how fo' do. Well, one pusson tell um say:

"'Make yo' mus' go to de country-fashion man. W'en he look de groun' he tell yo' wey t'ing kin do dat.[20]

"Den go to dat country-fashion man. Wen he look de groun' he tell dem, say, ef den wan' fo' ketch dah pusson wey (who) do dah trick, dem fo' get big wax,[21] make um lek young girl, en dis girl heah dey mus' put nah one co'ner inside de ho'se. So dey duh do all. Well, Spider no know anyt'ing happen. Wen de people done go, he come out soffle, lek wey he do de odder tem. He get de big, big pot, he was' um, put um nah fiah. He go take ress, he go cook de ress; den he take de pot, he pin (placed) um down 'pon de groun' close de fiah. He take odder leelee pot, he go look ef den get fis'; he fine leelee bit. He cook de fis' good fashion, make soup wid um. He pin de soup down close de ress. He go take de plate now, he was' um, but he no get 'tick-'poon[22] fo' dish up. He take 'tick wid fiah 'pon um fo' go look 'poon. Well, w'en he take de fiah-'tick, he see dis wax 'tan' up one side. He say: 'Eh! eh! Yo' bin heah so all de tem, en make me trouble fo' cook ress all, sotay I done cook de soup? Yo' no come se'f fo' he'p me?'

"De Country-fashion Man look de groun'."

"De t'ing no talk.

"'Well, now I done finish, go make yo' dish up de ress, make we yeat.'

"But w'en de t'ing no answer, Spider say:

"'How yo' kin do? I duh talk, yo' no hearee wey t'ing I duh say? I *say*, yo' mus' go pull dah ress, make we yeat.'

The Wax Girl.

"W'en de t'ing no duh talk, Spider hole um wid he han'. 'Jus he hole um, now he han' fash'n (stuck fast), he say:

"'Because I no hole yo' wid all two han', dat make yo' duh hole me tight?'

"W'en he hole um wid he odder han', he han' fash'n agin en he say:

"'Eh! eh! Lef me now! Ef yo' no wan' pull (bring) dah ress tell me, make me go pull um fo' mese'f. Yo' t'ink say nar (it is) play

I duh play? Fo' dat yo' kin do so? He look lek say yo' wan' make me kick yo'.'

"He kick um; he foot fash'n, he say:

"'Yo' make so I go kick yo' wid dis me odder foot jus' now.'

"W'en he take de odder foot, kick um, dat fash'n agin. He say:

"'Eh! eh! Ef yo' no lef me I go box yo' wid me head.'

"Den he butt um, en he head fash'n 'pon de wax.

"'Ef yo' no lef me, I go conk (strike) yo' jus' now wid me chest.'

"He conk um, he chest fash'n. W'en Spider he fine how he fash'n all, he begin fo' talk soffle, he beg, he *beg*, he say:

"'Lef me now, do yah. Soon do' go clean.'

"W'en he beg, de t'ing no duh talk: jus' 'tan' up deh. Spider fet, he fet, he *fet* t-a-y (till) do' go clean; he no come out. De mo' he duh fet de mo' he duh fash'n. He wef come out town, he come meet Spider, he say:

"'Ah! Fren', nar *so* yo' bin do all de tem? Aintee yo' say yo' duh die fo' make yo' take all de ress? Well, mese'f I no go lef yo' come out f'om dah place. Yo' fo' 'tan' up deh (there).'

"Spider 'tan' up dey tay (till) all de people to de town come meet um; dem beat um *fine*."

"Well, fus' tem Spider bin roun' lek pusson, but he fash'n so 'pon dah wax w'en den people all duh beat um, dat make he flat tay (till) to-day. Dis now de punishment he duh get. Story done."

The narrative of Mr. Spider's successive disasters with the Wax Girl moved forward with accelerated energy. Now and then came a brief pause to allow the story-teller to reinforce voice and tone with a fitting gesture, or to give vent to that peculiar, deep-throated chuckle which was his only outward evidence of inward delight. The eyes of the listeners danced and sparkled. They mimicked Spider's successive blows as the speaker illustrated them, and swayed to and fro, or shook with convulsions that threatened every minute to become uncontrollable. The last statements were uttered hurriedly, as if to give the pent up storm of laughter a chance to escape before it should work serious consequences. With the words "Story done," the men gave way to unrestrained and unrestrainable hilarity.

"He conk um, he conk um, he conk um," repeated Oleemah, in a voice choked with mirth, trying by the repetition to experience again all the delicious humor of the situation.

"He han' fash'n, he foot fash'n, he head fash'n, he chest fash'n," remarked Gondomah, while his whole frame shook with merriment, and the remark started a new fit of laughter.

Long after the noisy outburst had ceased, the comments continued concerning Mr. Spider's propensity for trickery, and his notorious capacity for "yeat."

It was not long before the tales were going again regarding some of Mr. Spider's numberless exploits. This time Oleemah was the story-teller. He had been sitting unusually silent for some time, but now, lifting his head and sniffing the air significantly, he remarked:

"One tem Cappen Spider, he en Lizzad make boat of Chameleon."

Here he paused, as if there were nothing more to say, but the men, scenting a story, urged him to go on. After a decent show of reluctance, he proceeded to tell how

## Mr. Chameleon Is Transformed Into A Boat.

"One tem Spider, Lizzad en Chameleon, dem t'ree beef bin meet up 'pon de road. Dey wan' go nah Freetown, but none no get boat fo' kare dem. So now dey go talk to dense'f who go be de boat. Well, dey come fine say, Chameleon, he go be de boat, because he favor boat. He han' nar de row-lock, heen tail wey fo' place de rudder, heen head nar de bow, de inside part fo' put de load. Chameleon 'gree. W'en dey ready fo' start, Chameleon say: 'Make I turn over; w'en I lay down flat, make yo' sit down 'pon me.'

"Spider say: 'All ret.'

"W'en he en Lizzad done klim 'pon dis boat-Chameleon, Chameleon say: 'Make Lizzad take dem hoe (oars).'"

Here Dogbah, who was rather slow of comprehension, interrupted with a question as to how Lizard was to use oars without row-locks.

Oleemah cast a disapproving glance at the questioner, then good-naturedly went on to explain what seemed to him self-evident. Holding up two fingers and a thumb as nearly in the shape of Chameleon's hand as possible, he said:

"Aintee yo' know Chameleon get two fingah en one t'umb so?" Lizzad put de hoe between um; he begin fo' pull, en dey begin fo' go. Spider nar de cappen; Lizzad dey take fo' boatman, because he kin pull wid he four foot.

"W'en dey go dey meet one place wey de stone plenty; Cappen Spider wey duh steer, he make de boat go agin de stone. So he duh do all tem, he jus' duh jam Chameleon 'pon dem stone. Chameleon done tire, he say: 'We no reach yet?'

"Spider say: 'We no half, yet.'

"Now he duh steer close one big, big rock, en de same tem Lizzad duh pull *hard*. Chameleon he back broosh 'pon stone, en he say: "Wee-ee! Fren', I no lek dah trick wey yo' do me to-day.'

"Spider make lek he sorry, he say: 'Fren', hush yah!'[23]

"So Chameleon lay down agin. Lizzad pull, he pull, he pull, he pull, he pull so-t-a-y (till) Chameleon ax um, he say: 'Wey t'ing do de place far so?'[24]

Mr. Chameleon transformed into a boat.

"Spider say: 'He no far agin; we go reach jus' now.'

"W'en dey go long tem, dey begin fo' see de town. Chameleon ax um agin, he say: 'Fren', we no reach yet?'

"Spider say: 'Look de town yandah.'

"Chameleon say: 'I no ax yo' fo' dat; I say, Ef we done reach dey?'

"Spider say: 'No, look de town yandah agin.'

"Chameleon say: 'Fren, I no lek dah trick. Tell me one tem ef we done reach dey.'

"Spider tell de same word agin, en Chameleon vex, he say 'I *mus'* come out jus' now under yo', make all man swim fo' hese'f.'

"Spider beg, he beg sotay (till) Chameleon say: 'All ret.'

"Den dey go agin, go reach de place, en Chameleon say: 'We done reach?'

"Spider say: 'Yes.'

"Chameleon ax: 'Ef make I turn over?'

"Spider say: 'No, come make yo' go to de sho' mo' leelee bit.' W'en dey reach to de sho,' Spider say: 'Turn over now, we done ketch Freetown.'

"Dis tem Chameleon get one foot en one han', en leelee nose, because Spider 'deed bin jam um 'pon dem stone. Dat make Chameleon walker slow tay to-day."[25]

Oleemah leaned back against the side of the boat, and gave himself up to a train of memories that had been awakened by the story just ended. The men, less meditative, renewed their enjoyment by various comments on Spider and his guileful ways.

"Aintee now dat rascal trick wey Spider do heen boat

Chameleon?" asked Dogbah, and his broad grin showed that Spider's rascality was not looked upon with any great disfavor. "Dat rascal trick" recalled the time when Spider was worsted in his encounter with the Wax Girl, and again the men shook with merry laughter.

Sobah, feeling a little hurt by some of the rude jests at Spider's expense, had been turning over the leaves of his memory in search of some exploit of that little hero, more than usually clever, in order to offset the somewhat inglorious part he had played in the two other tales.

"Well, Spider he 'trong man," he finally retorted to the slighting comment of Dogbah.

Challenged for proof of his assertion, Sobah began to relate Mr. Spider's marvellous achievement in a trial of strength with Elephant and Hippopotamus.

## Spider, Elephan' En Pawpawtámus.

"Hangry tem (famine) done ketch dis Africa.[26] All dem beef no get no yeat, de country dry too much. Well, Spider he en Elephan' meet up one day. Spider tell Elephan', 'How do.' Elephan' answer um, 'Tankee,' en he say:

"'Fren', how yo' do fo'get yeat? Mese'f no get notting, de country dry too much.'

"Spider hese'f done po'; hangry duh ketch um *bad*, but wey (since) he cunnie, he answer Elephan', he say:

"'Nar true de place dry, but I t'ink I go soon be able fo' fine yeat fo' mese'f en me famble.'

"Den de Elephan' say: 'Ef yo' fine de place, make yo' come tell me.'

"Spider say: 'All ret, I 'gree. I kin sorry w'en I look yo' skin, how he leelee so. He no big lek fus' tem; bimeby he no go big pass me yown. Yo' no look lek yo' get 'trenk too much; I t'ink say I able fo' draw yo' f'om de sho' to de wattah.'

"Elephan' no know say Spider duh pull cunnie, en hese'f de one Spider wan' fo' kill. He answer: 'All ret,' he say: 'Mese'f kin draw yo' f'om dah wattah to dah lan'.'

"Spider say: 'All ret,' he say he go fine big rope.[27] He go, he duh walker inside bush tay he meet rope big lek pusson head, he duh kare um go to de wattah. He 'tan' up close de sho' tay (till) he meet up wid Pawpawtámus, he tell um, say: 'I kin draw yo' f'om de wattah to de lan'.'

"Pawpawtámus say: 'Wey t'ing dat yo' duh talk? Yo' leelee too much, I jus' make me fingah *so*, I kin draw yo'.'

Mr. Spider challenges Pawpawtámus.

"Spider say: 'All ret, which tem we go try de fet?'

"Pawpawtámus answer um, say: 'To-morrow mawnin' make we come try.'

"Spider 'gree, he say: 'Dah tem I ready, I go gie yo' de rope.'

"Den he lef, he go tell Elephan' de same word: 'Wen I ready I go gie yo' de rope.'

"De two beef no know say dat dey two go draw each odder. So Spider bring de rope, he go tie de one end 'pon Elephan', de odder 'pon Pawpawtámus. He tell all two, he say:

"'Yo' mus' ready; I go draw yo' now.'

"So Spider hese'f go middle de rope, he begin fo' draw de rope to one side en de odder side fo' gie signal. Den he turn behine one big 'tick; he 'tan' up deh, fo' see wey t'ing go be. Dem two big beef begin fo' pull. Dey draw each odder sotay (until) dey no able; dey done tire fo' draw. De two equal, de one no pass he cumpin (companion) fo' 'trong. Dey draw sotay (until) dey all two die."

No mere words can convey an adequate impression of the realism and power that Sobah's portrayal gave to this mighty struggle. In unconscious response to the growing intensity of the theme he had risen to his feet, and now became so completely absorbed in the struggle he was depicting, that tone, look, and straining muscle seemed to reflect every phase of the terrible combat, until with the tiring out of the contestants, he too sank back upon his seat as if exhausted.

It was an effective bit of unstudied eloquence. The long pause that followed was necessary to allow the tension of feeling to sink again to the level of the remainder of the story. Then the narrator went on in a more subdued vein.

"Spider done satisfy. He look de beef, he say: 'Yo' pass me fo' 'trong, but aintee I pass yo' fo' sense?'

"Well, he go, he take dem two, he drag dem nah sho'."

This was a rather surprising feat even for Mr. Spider, and Sobah glanced out of the corner of his eye to see how it was being received. The look on several faces seemed to indicate that credulity was being tested too far. The momentary pause gave Oleemah a chance to protest: "Ah! Daddy, Yo' t'ink say Spider, wey leelee so, able fo' drag dem big, big beef?"

"Aintee yo' know dat Spider able fo' tote yeat?" Sobah replied. "Ef yeat big lek Elephan' he go tote um. I no care ef anyt'ing fo' yeat how he big, he kin hase (raise) um go, but he lazy fo' wuk. Ef yo' gie um leelee wuk fo' do, he no able." Then he resumed his narrative.

"Spider shabe (divided) de beef all; he call plenty people fo' tote um, kare um go nah he ho'se. He pay um only leelee bit 'pon dah Elephan'. Spider en he famble lib 'pon de two beef sotay de hangry tem done.

"Well, dah tern fis' no bin nah de whole wuld. W'en Spider shabe de beef, all de piece he no wan', he t'row 'way nah de wattah; den turn fis'. Nar so Spider make fis' all come nah de wattah."

This novel account of the "living creatures that the waters brought forth abundantly," did not seem incredible to that simple-minded crew. The water about their boat was alive with fish at the very moment, and if Spider did not make them, who did?

Hobahky, in whose nostrils the odor of fish-stew was a sweet savor, put his feelings into: "Aintee Spider good man fo' make dem fis' all come fo' we?"

Oleemah was inclined to give most credit to Spider for the

clever ruse by which he secured food for himself and family during the famine.

Meanwhile the wind had abated, and was shifting to a more favorable quarter. The clouds that had obscured the moon in the earlier evening, had cleared away, and now the moon was shining full and bright. Sobah's experienced eye had been taking in the situation, and after a full survey he decided that, after all, the voyage might safely be resumed.

Accordingly they set up their little mast, spread the sail, and were soon scudding away in the direction of Freetown, leaving thoughts of Spider to less strenuous hours.

## CHAPTER V

# A PURRO INITIATION

A short time after Sobah's return from his trading trip, occurred the initiatory mysteries of the Purro secret society. Nearly all the male population of the village had gone to the "devil-bush," or lodge of the society, to take part in the mystic ceremonies. A place had been hewn out of the dense forest, and across the front next to the village, was a barricade of bamboo fifteen feet high, with a single small opening covered by matting. Cabalistic symbols marked the presence of the Purro devil; and a long yellow snake, the guardian of the Purro society, was coiled up on the limb of a tree just inside the entrance. None but the initiated and the candidates dared to go within. Down in the village the women and children spoke with bated breath, and seldom ventured outside their huts. From the devil-bush came the dread rumble of the specially constructed drum, and the still more horrible call of the Purro devil. The air was full of dread, and awe, and mystery. Konah nestled close to her mother, not venturing even to ask questions. All at once the loud blare of some terrible instrument, heard from the edge of the village, and followed by the most hideous cry that ever came from human throats, told that the Purro devil was marching abroad, seeking new subjects for initiation. Konah and her mother, with some women and children who happened to be visiting them at the time, ran to the small inner room of their hut, and hid their faces against the dark wall. The uninitiated men who happened to be in the way, turned aside and buried their faces in their hands, that they might not look upon the dread Purro devil and his followers. On they came, the devil blowing his awful-sounding instrument, and the Purro boys uttering their terror-inspiring cry. The procession wound through the crooked streets, and passed on to the neighboring village. After the hideous noises died away, the women and children crept timidly out of hiding. The sun had gone behind the western forest, and Mamenah, Konah, and their visitors, came out to the front piazza, Mamenah seating herself in the hammock and the others upon the low mud wall.

The Purro Devil.

Konah's mind was full of Purro mysteries, but here was something which she dared not investigate personally. Her questions brought no satisfactory response, so she sat and pondered. Mammy Mamenah, wishing to entertain her friends, and at the same time to shake off her own uncanny feeling, finally asked:

"Yo' know dah trick wey Cunnie Rabbit pull (played), fo' blow all dem horn?"

They had not heard the story, but were at once ready to listen to it. At the first question, Konah was all eagerness and animation. Any story was delightful to her quick imagination, but the name of "Cunnie Rabbit" was a seductive charm beyond her power to resist.

"Oh Mammy, tell 'bout um," she ventured to request, and her voice was full of pleased anticipation.

Leisurely swinging in the hammock, Mamenah crooned her story in a tone more than usually subdued, for the echo of the Purro call was still fresh in her memory.

## Cunning Rabbit Becomes A King.

"All dem beef en Cunnie Rabbit bin meet up to one place. Now dey pull (removed) all dem horn, en put um 'pon de groun'. Any (every) beef pull he yown."

"How dem beef able fo' pull dem horn?" asked one of the children in a tone of incredulity.

"Dah tem wey de story bin tell 'bout, dem beef able fo' do anyt'ing; dey able fo' pull dem horn, dey able fo' take um agin.

Well, dah tem, dey pull dem horn all. One grain (single) pusson no lef' se'f wey (who) get horn, en dey say:

"'De pusson wey blow all dis yeah horn one (by) one, widout he no lef fo' blow, dis one we go take fo' king.'

"So Spider grap (get up), he blow de horn long, long tem, but bimeby he tire, he no done um, now he lef fo' blow.

"Elephan' grap, he say wey he big so, he go blow *all*.

"Cunnie Rabbit he say: 'Yo' duh story, yo' no able fo' do dis t'ing. Yo' see Spider wey duh pass yo' fo' cunnie, he no done dem; nar (is it) yo' go done dem?'

"Elephan' say: 'All ret, I go begin one tem (at once).'

"He blow sotay (till) he done part of dem plenty horn, but he no able fo' finis'; he lef fo' (left off) blow. Well, now all de odder beef duh try, dey all no able. Cunnie Rabbit grap (get up) en begin fo' blow, but wey (since) he cunnie, w'en he bin wan' lef (leave off), he bin pull one trick. Yo' know w'en dem Purro boy bin come nah town, to-day, w'en de debble bin talk en dey no wan' make people hearee, well, he make dem holler sotay he lef fo' talk, sometem 'bout t'ree minute.

"Well, Cunnie Rabbit, w'en he done tire, he look, he listen; he make lek pusson wey duh hearee somet'ing. Den he holler dis one big holler. De odder beef mean say de Purro boy duh come. Dey 'tan' up en holler one big, big holler tay all de groun' duh shake. Dey no take notice dat Cunnie Rabbit lef fo' blow. Well, w'en dey all stop fo' holler, he begin back fo' blow. W'en he done tire agin, he duh pull dis same sense; so he do t'ree tem, fo' make he get leelee tem fo' rest. Well, nar so he done all dem horn, en de beef take um fo' de king."

Cunnie Rabbit pretends to blow all the horns.

Konah was entirely satisfied with the success of her cunning little favorite, and for several minutes gave vent to a delighted chuckle. Presently the thought of Mr. Spider and his cleverness came into the mind of one of the women, and turning to Mamenah she asked for a story about him.

"I no able fo' 'member odder story," answered the woman doubtfully. The others, however, were not to be denied, so Mamenah began to stir the cobwebs of her memory to see if she could discover Mr. Spider and some of his doings. Her mind was still full of secret society initiations, and that probably was the reason why this particular experience of Mr. Spider was brought to the surface. Konah saw that a story was coming, so she came and curled up on a mat close to the hammock. The moon just then peeped over the tops of the trees, and shone full on the eager little upturned face waiting for the story to begin.

## Mr. Spider Initiates The Fowls.

"One tem fowl bin gadder all togedder." There was a tone of solemnity in the woman's voice when she made this simple introduction to her tale, a note which showed that her thoughts were more serious than if fowls were the only beings concerned. The child felt the change of tone at once, but merely leaned a little nearer, and listened more intently. In the same serious tone the story went on.

"One tem fowl bin gadder all togedder."

"Dey say dey wan' put Bundo,[28] but dey no get nobody fo' put dem Bundo. W'en dey duh talk dis word so, Spider come, he meet dem duh talk. He say, he go put de Bundo. He go to de town, he tell de chief he wan' to put all fowl Bundo. Now de chief say: 'All ret.'

"Spider tell de chief fo' sen' plenty man fo' buil' one big, big ho'se. Well, w'en dey done buil' dis ho'se heah, Spider say to de fowl:

"'To-morrow so, now make yo' se'f ready, oonah (you) all.'

"Now he go sharp he knef, Wahtah, wootah! wahtah, wootah! De fowl dey too plenty; dey get one town fo' demse'f, soso fowl (only fowls). Now Spider he sharp he knef good fashion, he come tell de fowl, he say:

"'Oonah go make de fench 'roun de ho'se, so nobody see de Bundo.'

"Well, w'en dey finis' buil' dis fench wid palm 'roun de ho'se, he tell de chief, say:

"'I wan' one big, big pot; I wan' plenty ress (rice) fo' de Bundo fo' yeat.'[29]

"W'en de chief done gie um all dis, Spider say:

"'I wan' plenty palm-ile, twelve jug[30] palm-ile.'

"Well, w'en de chief done gie um all dis, he ax Spider, say:

"'Wey t'ing yo' wan' agin? Talk, make I gie yo'.'

"Now Spider say: 'I wan' make de fowl gadder one place, make dem go inside de ho'se.'

"De chief say: 'Dis net heah I go sen' word.'

"Befo' de net done fa' down good fashion, w'en de place dark leelee bit, de chief heen (his) messenger walker all 'bout wid dis de chief heen command.[31] He tell de fowl all, make dem mus' gadder mawnin' early, make dem go inside de ho'se wey dey done buil' fo' um, make nobody no lef de town fo' go odder place.

"Nah (in the) mawnin' early, all dem fowl meet up one place; dey go inside de big, big ho'se, en Spider hese'f go inside. Ebery mawnin' Spider kill 'bout one t'ousan', he put um inside pot."

Konah's quick wit had anticipated Spider's selfish designs, but a thousand fowls for breakfast seemed such an enormous amount even for his notorious appetite, that she laughed outright at the absurdity of it.

The cunning scheme of Mr. Spider, hidden under a cloak of disinterested service, appealed more strongly to the woman, so she went on with a touch of irony in her voice:

"Nar dis de Bundo he duh put. He duh yeat all dem fowl him one (alone), he done um. Only leelee one wey duh hatch he lef.

"Nar de chief ax um, say: 'Which side yo' duh pull de Bundo?'[32]

"Spider tell de chief de place, den he say:

"'I wan' make yo' buy plenty dress fo' dem. Which tem yo' go buy de dress? Because I wan' pull de Bundo one tem, make I go.'

"Now the chief gie um all dem t'ing fo' dress dem; hankercher, bead, all t'ing wey kin tie nah han' nah foot, all t'ing de chief gie um.

"Well, w'en Spider done yeat de fowl, he pack de bone all one place. Now he tell de chief, he say:

"'To-morrow, w'en de sun middle de sky, I go pull de Bundo.'

"Well, dah net he gadder he pickin all, he say, make dem ready fo' go dis net.

"Well, all t'ing wey de chief gie Spider fo' de Bundo, he tie um in bundle, in mat; he gie um to he pickin (pickaninnies) fo' tote (carry); he lock de do' tight.[33] Now he tell de pickin, say:

"'Dis net yeah, make we come go, make we go walker all net; bimeby de chief go ketch we, go flog we.'

"Dey walker *all net*. Well, w'en do' clean, dey hide nah bush. Spider know dat Lepped inside dis bush, en Spider hese'f he 'fraid. Well, w'en de sun middle de sky, dat de tem fo' pull de Bundo, en plenty people duh gadder. Dey no see Spider nah de ho'se, so dey try fo' open de do'. Fus' dey no able; dey try long tem befo' dey open dis yeah do'. Now dey see dis great t'ing wey Spider done do. He pack de bone one side, he pack de fedder one side. Now de chief say make dem go ketch Spider. He sen' plenty pusson aftah um. Well, nar de Lepped holler inside bush, en Spider 'fraid bad; hese'f duh holler because 'fraid duh ketch um. W'en dem people hearee how Spider holler, dey know which side he duh hide, en dey go ketch um. W'en dey done ketch um, w'en dey done bring um nah de road, dey get de pickin all, but Spider he loss f'om dem han'. He go to one Mory[34] man, he tell um say:

"Make sebby (charm) fo' me, fo' make me joomp lek monkey.'

"De Mory man answer, he say:

"'Yo' mus' gie me one fine present fus'.'

"Now Spider tief plenty clot' en bead f'om de t'ing wey de chief gie um fo' pull Bundo. He gie um to de Mory man. Now de man make sebby, he tie um 'pon Spider. He tie one 'pon heen foot, he tie one 'pon de odder foot; one 'pon de han', one 'pon de odder han'. W'en he finis' he say:

"'Go show yo'se'f to de chief.'

"Well, w'en de chief see Spider, he tell de people, say:

"'Make all man mus' ketch Spider.'

"Dey dribe um, dey dribe um sotay (till) dey reach nah bush. Spider joomp nah 'tick, he joomp nah odder 'tick lek monkey. He bin get one sebby (charm) inside he han'. Dis he no fo' wop down. Ef he fo' get en wop um down, dat go make he lose he power fo' joomp lek monkey do, en de people dey go ketch um. *All day* dem people dribe um. W'en net come dey turn back, go nah town. Dey say dey done try all dem bes' fo' ketch Spider. Dey wan' ketch um, dey no able, because he duh joomp lek monkey. Nobody no able ketch monkey nah tree.

"Now all man duh hang head (think) fo' sabbee (know) wey t'ing dey go do fo' ketch Spider. At las' dey grap (get up), dey go to dis same Mory man wey Spider bin go to. He de bes' Mory man nah de wuld. W'en dey meet dis man, dey tell um all t'ing. Now de man say: 'Because oonah wan' ketch um, make oonah mus' gie me big, big present befo' I go gie yo' sebby (charm) fo' ketch Spider.'

"Now dey go get de present. He pass de one wey Spider gie, *far* 'way. Dey gie um to de man, en de man say:

"'Go ketch one black monkey, come bring me, but make he black fo' true.'

"Well, dey go make trap, dey go ketch dis black monkey heah, but he no die. Dey go gie um to de man. Now dis Mory man he make *one* sebby (charm), same wid Spider yown; he tie um 'pon dis monkey heen neck. He gie um good whip, fine one; de whip get six rope. He gie dis monkey sebben man, sebben 'trong man fo' wait tay he ketch Spider, so dey kin go tie um, bring um come to de chief. Five man no able hole um; because he get de five sebby, he get five man 'trenk.

"Well, now dis monkey hese'f grap, he go fo' ketch Spider. Spider se'f grap. He duh joomp, duh joomp, duh joomp sotay he t'ink dis black monkey yeah he no able fo' ketch um; dat make he no joomp lek wey he duh joomp befo'. Den de monkey he meet up wid um, he gie Spider one cut. Nar so dey do, dey joomp all day. De black monkey he follow behine Spider, he duh flog Spider ef he no joomp quick. Well, Spider he make hase (haste) agin; he joomp, he joomp, he joomp. Bimeby he go nah one rock place. De sebby (charm) wey he hole nah he han', de one wey he no fo' wop down, he take um, lay um 'pon de 'tone weh he sit down. He done lef dis monkey far distance, because he get five sebby; de monkey he only get one, so Spider joomp mo' pass monkey. He t'ink fo' say de monkey no meet um agin. He go nah one fa'm, he root cassada (cassava), he sit down 'pon rock, he yeat de cassada. Well, dis black monkey come up wid um. Spider no know; he duh yeat. Now de monkey flog Spider, he duh flog um. But Spider bin lef de sebby wey he get to he han', de sebby bin fa' down, so he no get 'trenk fo' joomp. He 'trenk inside de sebby. Now de monkey hole Spider sotay (till) de people reach de place. Spider look de sebby (charm) 'pon Monkey heen neck, he wan' take um. W'en he jog um fo' try pull um, Monkey no 'gree. Now dey tie Spider, dey kare um go to de chief. De chief put um nah prison, he deh four day, dey no duh gie um yeat. Well, Spider en Cunnie Rabbit bin fren; de one cunnie, de odder cunnie. Two cunnie meet up, dey two 'gree togedder. W'en net come so, Cunnie Rabbit go tief Spider nah prison. He get magic, he able go inside place wey (which) lock.

The Black Monkey starts after Mr. Spider.

"Mawnin', w'en dey go nah prison, dey no see Spider inside. Spider he free, he done go home back.

"So nar Spider bring tief long tem nah de wuld. He bin begin tief, so now we all duh tief."

Another of Mamenah's neighbors came in just here, with an interesting bit of news, and story-telling was at an end for this evening.

Konah still sat curled up on the mat, with her woolly head bent low, and her mind far away in fancy-land. Finally she crept inside the hut to her hard mud cot, and soon was flying before a black spectre that in the guise of a monkey kept pursuing her. Again she travelled a path with heaps of feathers on one side, and piles of bones on the other. Finally she lost the power to move, and felt herself bound and carried away to prison, and then in helpless loneliness she sobbed aloud. In the midst of her distress a kindly voice spoke: "Look me, I yo' fren', I go he'p yo' come out prison," and Cunning Rabbit stood beside her. With that her heart gave a bound of joy and relief, the troubled dreams fled, and sound sleep held her until the light of a new day drove away all the spectres of the night.

## CHAPTER VI

# THE BURNING OF THE FARM

THE day "fo' bu'n fa'm" had come. The thick underbrush of three or four years' growth had been laboriously chopped down by men and boys some weeks before and left in a tangled mass all over the little farm to become tinder for the flames under the burning sun of the long dry season now drawing to a close. Sobah had already postponed burning for several days longer than was necessary, for he had inherited the procrastinating tendency of his race, whose unwritten motto seems to be: "Do nothing to-morrow that can be put off until the day after to-morrow." This morning the sky was clear, and there was no excuse for further delay. Sobah, Mamenah and Konah started for the little piece of ground which had been allotted to them by the chief that year, going by the footpath which led from the village to the farm over the hill, a mile away. They had gone scarcely a third of the distance when Konah, who was running carelessly in advance, stumbled over an obstruction that happened to be lying in the road. This was a bad sign, and nothing would avert the evil consequences but a return to the village, and a roundabout journey by another road.

So they plodded back, and started once more by the longer way. Here a new difficulty presented itself. Just beyond the brook the path led beneath a tree under which a man had been killed by lightning some months before, and superstition invested the spot with special terrors. Sobah, however, knew the counter-charm, and plucking a leaf from a near-by shrub, cast it upon the place and passed on with an easy mind. Mammy Mamenah and Konah followed with the same precaution. The farm was reached without any other unfavorable signs. Some of Sobah's neighbors, earlier arrived, were engaged in burning an adjoining farm, and the air was heavy with the smoke and flying cinders. Fagots from the fire furnished torches by which Sobah's five-acre tract of dry brush was soon transformed into a lake of fire. The flames writhed and tossed angrily, like some great monster rushing to devour its prey. Konah was sure some devil was the animating power, and the uncanny movements of the fiery arms filled even the older ones with a feeling of awe and dread. It did not take the flames long to do their work in that dry fuel, and hardly had they died away when flocks of birds began to circle around the place, waiting for the fire to cool sufficiently for them to descend and enjoy their feast of roasted snails. Satisfied with their morning's work, Sobah, Mamenah, Konah, and the neighbors who had joined them in completing their labor, went to their farm-house to rest during the heat of the day, then to return to the village in the cool of the evening.

An hour's quiet repose made Konah's active nature eager for entertaining occupation. She climbed upon a large stone that lay at the shady side of the farm-house, and sat with one foot drawn up under her and the other dangling beside the stone, looking meditatively out over the blackness and smoke that told where the fire fiend had roared and revelled with resistless fury a little while before. The feeling still had possession of her that there was something more than natural in the way the fire had raged, and to her mind the supernatural was to be accounted for by multitudinous devil and witch influences. With her mind full of such thoughts, she was delighted to hear one of the men putting to Sobah the very questions that were crowding her own mind. "Oh, debble any place," he explained in reply. "He deh nah cotton-tree, he deh nah bush, he deh nah wattah, he deh nah groun'. He able fo' turn anyt'ing; he turn stone, he turn tree, he turn pigeon, he turn pusson. Pusson kin buil' debble-ho'se, put med'cin' inside wey dribe debble way f'om fa'm, en wey make he get good heart fo' um. Ef he get good heart, he no go do um bad. Notting no able fo' do um bad."

This to Konah's mind, bound in the universal network of superstition, was undisputed fact. Had she not in each transit to and from the farm, passed a tiny devil-house, placed on the outskirts of her home village? This presented itself now to her mind's eye: Four sticks driven into the ground, supporting a frame three feet square, roofed with bamboo, and enclosed on three sides. The fourth, left open, revealing a devil in the form of a small stone, a little food near by, the skull of some small animal, a bottle, a little horn, and some mysterious medicine tied in a very dirty rag.

The child had never questioned very deeply the significance of each article, taking the whole by faith as one accepts the religion of his ancestors, but her developing mind now longed to interrogate her father, who, she was sure, must be able to explain everything. This, however, she dared not do, for it was not a child's place to presume; neither did she care to incur a testy command to be silent, or to run away and do some work. The reproof she would not so much have minded, being used to it; but idleness was even sweeter than appeased curiosity. So she absent-mindedly picked little pieces from the stone on which she was sitting, and wondered, until presently Sobah, feeling that he had explained matters sufficiently for any reasonable purpose, had given himself over to the train of thoughts which his talk had set in motion, and was ready to tell a story in which Spider and "debble" were concerned. There was no announcement of the fact, yet by some occult means everyone knew that the proper time had arrived, and quite spontaneously turned to listen. A glance at the faces of his audience was all the encouragement the most exacting story-teller could require, and Sobah was really fond of being the mouthpiece for the yarns that Spider spun. The tale embodied some of the unseen powers that they had been discussing a few minutes before.

## Spider Tries To "Brush" The Devil's Farm.

"One tem Spider he go to 'trange lan'. Well, w'en he reach deh, he go to de king. De king nar he lan'lord. W'en tem reach fo' brush fa'm, he ax de king fo' one piece lan' wey de people nebber brush. Dey say one big debble get de lan', en no man no venture fo' go deh. Spider ax de king fo' dis same spot, he say he wan' fo' brush deh. De king he tell um, he say:

"'Nobody wey brush deh kin bring de ress (rice) nah town, he no go even yeat de ress.'

"Spider say: 'Me go yeat um; I go brush deh, en I go yeat de ress.'

"De king say: 'Well, all ret;' he say. 'Try yo' bes'.'

"Spider he bring cutlass,[35] he go early in de mawnin' fo' go commence brush befo' de sun hot. W'en he go he jus' duh chop one 'tick, den he hearee de debble ax:

"'Who chop dah 'tick?'

"De pot begin fo' run f'om Spider."

"Spider say hese'f duh chop dah 'tick.

"Den de debble say: 'By to-morrow yo' go meet I done brush all dis bush heah.' He tell Spider make he no brush, because he go brush fo' um.

"Spider go fo' drink wattah nah de fa'm-ho'se. Befo' he come back he meet de bush already brush. He run go nah town, he tell de king, he say:

"'I done finis' brush de fa'm wey yo' gie me.'

"De king answer, he say: 'All ret.'

"Befo' one week tem, de place all done dry fo' burn. Nex' day w'en de sun all done hot, Spider he go, he set de fiah, he holler, he say: 'Hey! hey! hey!' He do dat fo' make de debble go hear um, so de debble go ax lek how he duh do befo'. Den de debble ax, he ax: 'Who dat duh bu'n fa'm?'

"Spider answer um lek he bin do befo'.

"Den de debble say: 'Go sit down, I go bu'n um jus' now fo' yo'.'

"Soon w'en Spider go look, he see de fa'm done bu'n all, he swep' clean.

"Spider go tell de king, he say: 'I done bu'n me fa'm.'

"De king say: 'All ret.'

"He tell de king, he say: 'Buy ress fo' me.'

"De king gie um few hamper ress. Spider make hoe; long, long one. Nah mawnin' tem he get up, he take de ress, he go nah fa'm early, befo' do' clean. W'en he reach to he fa'm, he put down he bly (basket), he take he han', he dip de ress wid um, he hebe (scatter) um, schar-r-r!

"Now de debble ax um, he say: 'Who hebe de ress?' He say: 'I go hebe de ress, make de pusson no humbug,[36] I go hebe de ress jus' now.'

"But de Spider he no see de debble, he jus' duh see de wuk done, en jus' duh hear de voice, but he no duh see nobody. W'en he 'tay leelee bit, Spider he see ress all 'pon de groun'. Spider take de hoe, he scrape de groun', har-r-r!

"W'en de debble he hear, he say: 'Who duh dig de groun' fo' cover de ress?'

"He say: 'Go home;' he say: 'To-morrow mawnin' yo' go meet I finis' de place.'

"Spider go, he tell de king, he say 'I finis' plant me ress.'

"De king say: 'All ret.'

"Spider go back agin to de fa'm, he meet de ress already done grow, done high, he meet de grass begin fo' grow middle de ress. He go fo' root de grass f'om dah ress; he root one de grass; he root um *hard*, so de debble kin hear. De debble he ax: 'Who root de grass?' He say: 'Befo' evenin' tem de pusson go meet I root all de grass.'

"Spider go to de fa'm-ho'se wey he sit down. Evenin' tem he come out to de fa'm, he walk all 'bout, he see de fa'm clean. De ress he *fine*!

"Bimeby de tem reach fo' de ress fo' begin bear, de ress done bear all; dem bird dey duh come fo' yeat de ress. Spider w'en he meet de bird, he holler, 'Shoo! shoo!' Dem bird dey all get up, dey fly.

"Den de debble ax um, he say: 'Who duh dribe dem bird?' He say: 'De pusson no need fo' dribe de bird, I go dribe dem f'om de ress.'

"De debble he dribe dem bird ebery day f'om de ress, tay de ress all done ripe fo' cut. De fus' day Spider go cut some. Yo' know de fus' day pusson kin cut leelee fo' yeat, dat all. [37]W'en he go cut de ress, he go parch um, dry um to de pot; he beat um. He done beat de ress all, he begin fo' cook, he put big ress nah fiah fo' cook um, he cook all. Aftah he put de pot nah fiah, en de wattah in de pot done w'am nuff, he put de ress inside de pot. Jus' de ress done, he take de pot, pin um down close de fiah. Spider he go huntin', he kill bush beef, he cook um. Aftah de soup finis', he pull um f'om de fiah, he go was' dem dish fo' come take up. Spider come fo' touch de pot wey get de ress. De pot begin fo' run f'om Spider. Spider run aftah de pot, he duh *run*, duh *run*, duh *run*, duh *run*! Spider done tire, he stop fo' run, he 'tan' up; de pot se'f 'tan' up. W'en Spider 'tan' up, de pot stop fo' run. W'en he see dat de pot stop fo' run, well, him begin fo' run, fo' go take de pot quick.

W'en Spider reach close de pot, de pot begin 'gain fo' run. Spider en de pot duh run sotay (till) Spider he tire; he lef en go back nah fa'm-ho'se, he go sit down. He stay leelee bit, he see dah empty pot come back inside de fa'm-ho'se en 'tan' up. Spider no know how fo' do; he sorry, he wan' fo' cry. He say: 'But nebber min', I tink odder sense wey I go do bimeby, evenin' tem.'

"He stay hungry all day. Evenin' tem he cook de ress; he no even wait fo' de ress fo' finis' cook, he make big cottah,[38] he put um 'pon he head; he take de pot, he hase um up, put um 'pon he head; he tie de pot all wid rag 'roun' he head, fash'n um so he no able fo' loose. He start wid run fo' go nah town. De ress duh boil de same tem dat he duh run. Jus' he wan' fo' reach de town, de pot slip 'way f'om um. He begin fo' run aftah de pot, en de pot duh run tay Spider give up, he done tire. W'en he stay leelee bit, he see de empty pot agin. Spider, because he no get ress, he 'bliged fo' go pick de leelee young cassada; he cook, he yeat um.

"De nex' day, de same; he get de same trouble tay he gie up de fa'm altogedder, en go home.

"De king ax um, he say: 'Spider, how he 'tan'? Dat word wey I bin tell yo', dat nar (is it) story?'

"He answer um, he say: 'No, nar true word dat yo' bin talk, but nebber min'.'

"De king ax um, he say: 'Dah ress, yo' bin cut all?'

"He say: 'Yes, I done cut all de ress, he deh 'pon top de fa'm-ho'se wey I pile um.'

"De king he say: 'Yo' see 'trong head (obstinacy) no good, yo' labor fo' notting.'

"Spider he bin get 'trong head, dat make he bin see all dis trouble."

Konah followed the story through with intense interest, too absorbed to ask questions, even if she had dared. A rice pot that could perform such feats, was an entrancing object to her imagination. So delighted was she with the magical powers that were manifest in the story, that she forgot to hear the moral of the tale regarding obstinacy and self-will. Sobah, however, was so impressed with the application of the story, that he plunged into the recital of another tale teaching the same moral, and with a much more tragic outcome.

## The Devil Turns Pigeon

"One big debble ho'se bin close by one town. Dem debble wey bin deh, dem bad. Dey say: 'Make nobody no fo' set trap inside de bush.' So one 'tranger come to de town. All man tell um say: 'No fo' set trap inside dah bush (forest),' but he deny; he make 'tronger head, he say he mus' set trap deh. So he go make trap. W'en he set dis trap inside de bush, soon one pigeon go inside de trap. Dis bird nar debble wey bin turn bird en go inside de trap. De bird begin cry, he say: 'Daddy, come loose me.'

"So de 'tranger go loose de pigeon, he put um one side. De pigeon cry agin, he say: 'Daddy, kare me go nah ho'se. (De pigeon duh say so).'

"So de man take de pigeon, he kare um go nah ho'se.

"De pigeon cry: 'Daddy, kill me one tem.'

"W'en de man done kill um, he say: 'Daddy, pull de fedder 'pon me.'

"W'en de man done pull de fedder, de pigeon say: 'Clean me.'

"W'en he done clean um, de pigeon say: 'Put pot nah fiah.'

The Devil turns Pigeon.

"W'en he done put de pot, de pigeon say: 'Cut, cut me.'

"W'en de man done cut um, he say: 'Put me nah pot, cook me one tem.'

"Den de man cook um.

"Now de pigeon say: 'Daddy, put salt,' en he put salt. He say put peppy, en he put peppy. So de pigeon say: 'Tase de salt, ef he go do nah de soup.' Now de pigeon say de soup done. W'en he done cole, de pigeon say: 'Pull me, make yo' yeat me.' Well, w'en de man yeat um he lef half. De pigeon say: 'Yeat me all.' He yeat all.

"Evenin' tem de man go nah bush agin. Jus' he reach nah bush, he open he mout' fo' talk. Jus' he open um de bird fly f'om he mout' go 'way, en hese'f fa' down, he die. W'en de people look fo' um all inside de bush, dey no see um, de debble done kare um go.

"So deny no good. Ef pusson tell yo' say: 'No do dis t'ing, yo' no mus' make 'tronger head."

The dreadful consequences that might be expected to follow upon a headstrong course, Sobah set off with solemn look and awed tone; then shaking his head warningly, he concluded with the proverb: "Ef yo' wan' yeat out de debble he yown bowl, make yo' get 'poon wid long handle."

The story echoed a feeling of universal childhood, the undefined dread of some mysterious visitation upon disobedience and kindred sins that finds expression in the goblin stories of all tongues.

Konah felt it keenly, being impressed as much by the solemn manner of the recital, as by the matter of the story.

The older ones too, being but grown up children, were filled with much of the same vague awe, but years had dulled the keenness of their spiritual sensibilities. After some desultory talk on less serious matters, the men stretched out on the floor of the hut, and were soon asleep.

## CHAPTER VII

# MAMMY MAMENAH AND HER FRIENDS

ONE evening, about a week after the burning of the farm, a little company of women and children, in varying degrees of undress, was gathered in the larger room of Mamenah's hut. A fire had been kindled in the middle of the earthen floor; for the first showers, forerunners of the coming rainy season, had fallen. The children amused themselves as inclination led them, with sports ranging from gentle kitten-like romps, to a genuine fight, with biting, scratching, and hair-pulling accompaniments.

There was evident among the women, a feeling of abundant leisure, and of relaxation from responsibility. The "planting" of the rice had been completed. The seed had been scattered over the lately burned ground, had been rudely scratched in with a very primitive hoe, and was now awaiting germination under the moisture of the oncoming rains, and the warmth of occasional sunshine.

So the women felt free to spend the hours in gossip, and in the telling of tales. They chatted about personal matters, about the rice just planted, and then about the precautions taken to ward off evil influences, and to secure favorable conditions for their crops.

Mammy Mamenah told what a tempting bowl of rice she had prepared and offered to the spirit that dwelt in the big cotton tree near the corner of the farm, in order to enlist his kindly offices in guarding the rice field.

Mammy Yamah had set up a stick at the edge of her farm, and placed on top of it a bit of medicine wrapped in a leaf, which she had secured for an exorbitant fee from a medicine man. She was sure that anyone daring to molest would fall in spasms and die. Each had some specific with which to avert harm, or to secure favor.

Mammy Magbindee had a bit of news that made Konah's eyes dilate with wonder. It had been told in the village that very day by a person who had it from one who saw the mound, and of course it was true. Besides such occurrences had often been known before, and could not be doubted. A rich man had died in an adjoining town a few years before, and had been fittingly buried. Just now the grave had been accidentally opened, and strange to relate, it was found that gold had grown out of the ears of the man, and kept on growing until it filled the whole grave. But of course gold grows this way, for gold is in the world, and if it does not grow, where does it come from? Freaks of Nature can have but one cause, the presence of some "devil," and this thought reminded Mammy Mamenah of an old legend regarding another marvel of nature, which she proceeded to relate much to the delight of the whole company.

## A Stone That Wore A Beard.

"One day Spider go fo' set trap inside one big bush (forest). He meet one big stone wey duh get plenty bear'-bear'.[39] Dis not to true stone, he nar one debble wey bin turn stone."

A prolonged "Y-a-h-oh!" of assent from the women squatted about on the floor, accompanied by the swaying of bodies, and the exclamation from some one: "Nar true word yo' duh talk," showed how heartily they believed in the power of their devils to assume any form they willed, in order to carry out their purposes. It was a sympathetic audience that followed the remainder of the story. The children were listening open-eyed in silent eagerness. Mamenah went on impressively.

The Stone with the Beard.

"Ef pusson say de stone get bear'-bear' (beard), he go fa' down de same place close de stone, he go wan' die. So one day, w'en Spider go set trap to dis place, he meet de stone. Now he say: 'L-a-w-cus! Dah stone get plenty bear'-bear'.' So he fa' down de same place. He no able fo' grap (get up) all day. W'en at las' he betty leelee bit, he go home.

"Spider wan' fo' make cunnie fo' yeat he cumpin (companion), en he come fin' out say dis plan go be fine fo' get um. So one day he go to Deer, he tell um, say:

"'Fren, come go follow me, I go look me trap.'

"Deer say: 'All ret.'

"All two dey walker half way, den Spider say:

"'Deer, make yo' go befo', I go show yo' de road; de road nar dis.'

"W'en dey done reach close de stone, Spider 'tan' up, he wait. Deer go, him too big fool, him say: 'L-a-w-cus! Look dah stone, he get plenty bear'-bear'.'

"Nar so he fa' down deh, he wan' die. Spider make hase come cut he t'roat, he kare um go, he en he pickin en he wef. Dey yeat de Deer all.

"De odder tem he go call Feleentambo (gazelle), he say: 'Fren', come go follow me, I go set me trap.'

"So w'en dey duh go, he 'tan' up one side, he tell Feleentambo make he go befo'. W'en Feleentambo go he see de stone, he no keep he mout', he say: 'Dah stone get plenty bear'-bear'.' So he fa' down deh. Spider run, he cut he t'roat.

"Nar so he do *all* dem odder beef. At las' he go call Cunnie Rabbit, he say: 'Fren', come go follow me to me trap.'

"Well, dey go. W'en dey reach close de stone, Spider 'tan' up, he say: 'Fren', pass befo', look de trap ef he ketch.'

"Cunnie Rabbit go befo', he go see de stone heah, but he silence. Spider wait, he wait fo' hearee ef he go talk, but he no talk. So he call Cunnie Rabbit, he say: 'Wey t'ing yo' see?'

"Cunnie Rabbit say: 'I no see anyt'ing.'

"Spider tell um, say: 'Yo' no see yandah to dat stone?'

"Cunnie Rabbit say: 'Wey t'ing?'

"Spider put he han' to he chin, he say: 'Yo' daddy no get so?'

"But Cunnie Rabbit get sense, he no talk, so Spider tell Cunnie Rabbit: 'Make yo' mus' say "Stone get pl——"

"Cunnie Rabbit hese'f say: 'Stone get pl——'

"Spider vex, he say: 'Ah, me fren', yo' stupid! Make yo' mus' say: 'Dah stone get plenty b—'

"Well Cunnie Rabbit say: 'Dah stone get plenty b—'

"Spider say: 'Ah, me fren', yo' no kin say de stone get plenty bear'-bear'?'

"So Cunnie Rabbit hese'f say so, en dey all two fa' down de same place. Dey wan' fo' die, dey no able fo' grap (get up). Nar deh, Trorkey go meet dem. Well, because Cunnie Rabbit bin good pusson, Trorkey he hase (raise) um up, en Cunnie Rabbit go 'way. Trorkey say: 'I bin go lif' yo', Spider, but bimeby yo' go lie 'pon me; yo' go say yo' fine Trorkey fa' down so heah, en yo' se'f bin he'p um.'

"Spider say: 'No, I no go do so.' He beg Trorkey sotay (till) Trorkey he'p um, he hase um up.

"F'om dat day Cunnie Rabbit get sense. Spider hese'f no able um,[40] he pass all odder beef."

A delighted little exclamation from Konah greeted this praise of her Cunnie Rabbit. For several minutes after the close of the narrative, there was an indistinguishable jabber of voices, all eager to add some "debble story", if possible more exciting than the one just told.

Finally Mammy Magbindee gained the right of way, and her story was:

## The Girl That Plaited The Devil's Beard.

"One tem debble bin sit down to de road-side. Any pusson wey bin go nah dat road, de debble bin yeat um. Well, one day, one girl say:

"'I go kill to-day dis debble heah.'

"W'en he go he meet de debble, he duh sleep close de road-side. De debble get long bear'-bear' (beard). De girl go soffle, he hole de bear'-bear', he duh plant (plait) um. Den he draw de debble go nah town. He draw um, he draw um tay de people inside de town hearee wey de girl duh draw um, en wey de debble duh sing:

"Tittie (sissy) duh kare me bear'-bear',
Tittie duh kare me bear'-bear'.'

"W'en de people hearee um, den go he'p de girl fo' draw. Dey go put de debble nah big road en kill um. W'en dey done kill um, dey wan' 'plit um, but somet'ing no bin deh fo' take. One leelee prophet bird[41] come nah bush, he say:

"'Oonah mus' take dah leelee sharp t'ing nah bush (thorn), oonah kin 'plit um.'

"De debble, he duh sleep close the road-side."

"Now dem people take dah bird, dey fling um far 'way, but he come agin back, he say:

"'Oonah take dah leelee sharp t'ing nah bush, 'plit um.'

"Dey fling um agin, but de bird come back agin en sing de same sing. Dah tem wey make t'ree, dem people say:

"'Make we try ef de t'ing true wey de bird bin talk; ef so, we go make um fine present.'

"Den dey go take de sharp t'ing. W'en dey jus' touch de debble heen body so, he 'plit. Wen he 'plit, all den people come out; dey no bin die, dey bin make fa'm inside de debble; dey bin bu'n fa'm, make ho'se, dey duh cook, dey duh yeat. W'en he done 'plit, all man come out, plenty people come out."

Neither story-teller nor listeners realized that there was anything preposterous in such a being as the one here described. On the other hand, the gasps and groans that greeted each startling revelation, contained not a tinge of incredulity, but only a kind of reverence for this supernatural capacity so in accord with their conception of spirits and devils.

The several steps leading up to the climax, were rolled off in rapid succession; "W'en dey touch heen body so, he 'plit, w'en he 'plit all dem people come out, dey no bin die, dey bin make fa'm inside de debble, dey bin bu'n fa'm, buil' ho'se, dey duh cook en yeat; plenty people come out," yet each was rounded off with such peculiar emphasis of tone and gesture, that it came with a distinct impression of its own, only heightened by the cumulative effect of succeeding revelations.

A pause of several minutes was necessary before the story could proceed.

"Well, one ole granny, w'en he come out, he say:

"'I fo'get me leelee pot, en me pickin, en me med'cin'.'

"Dem people say: 'No go agin inside dis debble heah!'

"He answer um back, say: 'I mus' go.'

"W'en he go inside, now de t'ing shut.

"Dis tem de bird done fly go, den done present[42] um money en plenty fine t'ing. Dey try fo' 'plit de debble agin, lek how dey bin do fus' tem, but dey no able, because de bird bin *make* um open de fus' tem. Wey t'ing fo' do? Dey try all kin' of sharp t'ing nah dis wuld, but den no able. Dey go bury de debble so.

"Dat make 'tronger head no good. Ef pusson tell yo' say, make yo' no mus' do anyt'ing, no do um."

Others were eager to relate stories to match the ones already given, but quite naturally and woman-like, the one all were most ready to hear was the one that smacked of romance, and promised to recount the uncanny courtship and marriage of a beautiful young girl and the devil. It was Yamah, the youngest woman present, who told the story, and she told it with an earnestness that might have sprung from personal experience.

## Marry The Devil, There's The Devil To Pay.

"Now one day, one mammy get girl pickin (pickaninny). Dis pickin he too fine. Dem rich people en eberybody go ax fo' um fo' married, but he no 'gree. One rich man he deh down, down, *down* (south), he get plenty hoss, plenty people, plenty goat, en plenty t'ing wey I no able fo' talk. Dis man come fo' see de girl he people, so he go get de girl, but w'en de people tell dis girl, he no 'gree. De mammy bin tell de girl, say:

"'Anybody yo' see wey (whom) yo' lek, anyt'ing wey (which) yo' see I go kill um fo' present um. But de girl no see, anybody wey (whom) he (she) lek.

Marry the Devil, the Devil to pay.

"One day dah big, big, big, big debble, nah dah big, big bush, he hearee dis news, fo' say nobody no able fo' get dis girl heah, en dis debble he say: 'Nar me go married dis girl.' He grap, he go fix hese'f good fashion lek pusson. Aintee yo' know say debble he able make hese'f fine? He able fo' make hese'f fine pass anybody nah dis wuld. He put on all de bes' clot' wey he kin get fo' len' (borrow). He len' half side[43] head, half side body, all t'ing half side. So w'en dis debble finis' fix hese'f good fashion, he call he hammock en four man fo' tote (carry) um. He tell one man wey he lef' nah ho'se say: 'I duh go married,' en he start fo' come see dis girl heah. W'en he come, he reach nah de town wey de girl bin deh. De girl duh 'tan' up close de windah, he duh look de road. W'en he see dis man yeah duh come, he tell he mammy, say: 'I done see pusson wey I lek, nar he go marry me.'

"W'en de debble come close de ho'se, de girl go meet um, he bring um come inside.

"De debble say: 'I come fo' marry to yo'.' De girl say: 'All ret.'

"Now de girl go tell he mammy, he say: 'Mammy, dah cow wan' die.'

"Now de mammy say: 'Kill um fo' yo' man.'

"Now de girl say: 'Mammy, dem fowl dey sick.'

"De mammy say: 'Kill um fo' yo' man. Anyt'ing yo' wan', take um.'

"Dis girl yeah, w'en he go cook de beef en de fowl, wid ress en plenty odder t'ing, he go gie um to de man nah heen ho'se.[44] But dis debble yeah, he nebber yeat ress oh, he jus' duh yeat pusson, he nebber yeat odder t'ing. W'en dis girl bin kare dis yeat nah debble heen ho'se, w'en dah girl done go, de debble dig nah fireside, he put all dis ress inside dah hole, he cover um. Bimeby de girl come, he t'ink say de man jus' yeat leelee bit, he ax um, say:

"Wey t'ing yo' no duh yeat fo'?'

"De debble say: 'I done yeat plenty.' But dis girl he (she) no know dis nar debble, oh!

"Well, dis girl heah, he get one brudder wey sick wid craw-craw; craw-craw[45] 'pon heen skin all. Dis boy wan' go tell dis debble 'How do'. W'en he go, dis debble holler 'pon um. De boy 'fraid, he go sit down.

"Well, dis debble wan' pass go home. De girl say he no go lef, he mus' go wid de man. Heen people dey no 'gree make he go yet, but he say he mus' go now, so dey say: 'All ret.'

"Dey gie um all t'ing fo' make um go. Dis same day dey lef de town fo' go home. W'en dey go, dis boy wey (who) sick wan' fo' follow um. He say he mus' follow he sister, but de debble no 'gree, he say because de pickin too waw-waw (ugly).

"So w'en dey go, dah pickin duh follow um leelee (at a distance). Well, dey walker all day. W'en de debble turn, he see dis pickin yeah, he ketch um, he flog um, he say: 'No go follow we!'

"So de pickin go hide behine leelee bit, en de two pusson dey duh go. Soon de debble duck heen han' nah heen pocket,[46] he pull one white kola,[47] he open um; he gie de girl half, hese'f take half.

"De pickin come meet dem agin. W'en de man wan' flog de pickin de ooman say: 'Fren', no flog um, make he follow we.' 'Den de pickin follow leelee, leelee. Well dey walker all day. W'en dey go, dis debble heen one side head come out, fa' down. Well dis girl yeah say: 'Fren', look, yo' head fa' down.'

"Well, de debble pull one sing:
'Lef um deh (there), lef um deh, Berkinee;
Lef um deh, oh Berkinee.'"

The song, a weird chant in the minor key, had a slow swinging movement, and the whole company beat time with hand-claps, bringing the right hand down slowly upon the left, and swinging the body in unison. The song was given as a chorus, and served to quicken feeling and to intensify the interest of the story. When it was ended, Yamah proceeded:

"Dey go sotay (till) de one foot fa' down. De girl call um back, he say: 'Fren', yo' foot fa' down.'

"Den de debble pull de same sing:

'Lef um deh, lef um deh, Berkinee;
Lef um deh, oh Berkinee.'

"Aftah he done finis' sing, dey go sotay (till) all t'ing nah heen skin lef half. Dey reach evenin' tem nah (to) de man heen place, en dey come see dis leelee brudder. Den cook, den yeat.

"Well, de net, w'en dis heen (his) wef done sleep, dis debble grap fo' kill um, fo' yeat um. He take one big, big knef, he duh sharp um. But dis pickin yeah, he no sleep, he jus' duh make lek pusson duh make nah net (snore). W'en de debble finis' fo' sharp he knef, de pickin cry: 'W-e-y-ee! Me craw-craw duh kratch me oh?'

"Den de debble come to um, he say: 'Pickin, yo' no sleep yet?'

"De pickin duh say: 'No, sah, me craw-craw duh hurt me, en me nebber sleep 'pon bed. I ken lay down 'pon pile country clo'es.'[48]

"De debble go bring plenty country clo'es, he make fine bed fo' um. He put de pickin deh, make um sleep, so he kin yeat dis ooman. But dis ooman duh sleep oh! He duh sleep, he no know anyt'ing wey duh go on.

"Well, de man mean say de pickin done sleep, en he take he knef, he duh sharp, sharp um, make he come broke de ooman he head. He say: 'Fo' yeat pusson, he good, he sweet, en dis ooman he fat.'

"But dat pickin no sleep oh! He cough en de debble say: 'Pickin, yo' no sleep yet?'

"De pickin say: 'No, sah, hangry done ketch me.'

"De pickin know say dis man wan' yeat dah ooman, so he duh try make he mus' get some way fo' sabe um (save her); dah make he duh talk all light t'ing yeah. W'en dah debble gie um yeat, he go put de pickin agin nah de bed, make he lay down sleep. De tem nar middle net. Well, dis man yeah, w'en he done sit down long tem, he mean say de pickin done sleep. He take he knef agin, he sharp um. Now de pickin duh kratch, kratch he skin. De debble hebe he knef down quick, he go ax de pickin: 'Wey t'ing make yo' no sleep yet? Wey t'ing dey kin do fo' yo' craw-craw w'en yo' bin deh to yo' Mammy?'

"De pickin say: 'Dey kin take fis'-net, go take wattah nah wattah-side fo' was' um. I wan' was', but I nebber was' wid wattah wey dey bin get nah bowl, excep' de wattah fus' inside fis'-net, befo' dey turn um nah de bowl.'

"So de debble he grap (get up), he go nah wattah-side, he kare fis'-net en bowl. W'en he duh duck de fis'-net inside wattah so, en he hase de fis'-net, de wattah all lef back. Because he wan' hurry yeat de ooman, he stupid; he no wait t'ink he no able get wattah wid fis'-net. De pickin bin ax dis t'ing wey hard fo' do, fo' make leelee chance fo' sabe de ooman. He wake de ooman, he say: 'Yo' no know dat debble wan' kill yo' dis net yeah? Nar lie I tell um, say he mus' get wattah wid fis'-net befo' I kin was'. He done go. Grap (get up), make we come go; ef no so, ef he meet yo', he go kill yo'.'

"Dis boy yeah en dis ooman dey start, dey walker hard dah net. Well, dah debble, w'en he no able get dis wattah, he come nah ho'se, he meet de ooman en de pickin done go. So he run go follow dem. He walker sotay he wan' go meet dem, but dis pickin hearee de debble duh come behine, he say: 'Come hide!' So dey hide. De debble go sotay he wan' reach nah town, but he no meet dem, so he come back. Dis ooman en de pickin pass, go home.

"De girl tell him people all t'ing wey he see, he say: 'Trongah yase (ears)[49] no good. Ef I bin hearee oonah (you) w'en yo' bin say make I no go wid dis man, I no fo' see all dis trouble yeah'.

"So now he make *so*. Ef yo' wan' go any place, ef any pickin wan' follow yo', no deny. Sometem (perhaps) dis pickin yeah go sabe yo' f'om big, big trouble."

By the time this story was ended, most of the children were asleep, but Konah's insatiable hungering after the strange and mysterious, kept her wide awake. Some of the women, too, were beginning to feel the drowsy effects of the night, and especially of the close, smoke-laden air within the over-crowded little room.

Magbindee went to the door, and seeing the moon just then peeping through a rift in the clouds, rudely awoke her sleeping child, and started with it to her own hut.

Others followed her example, and soon Sobah's hut was left to stillness and to dreams.

## CHAPTER VIII

# CHILDREN OF NATURE

NATURE is very human in many of her moods. She has her periods of feverish energy and impetuous application, then her periods of gentle outpouring and watchful tenderness, and again her periods of apparent idleness and indifference. In Temne-land these moods succeed each other with a regularity and certainty that is quite pronounced. The dry season just ended, was the period of repose and idleness. Nature had been taking her vacation. The currents of life stood still, and vegetation sank into a partially dormant state. Nature, resting, seemed forgetful of her human children. Day after day, week after week it had been the same,—sunshine, profuse, clear, steadfast and pitiless; air quiet and calm and listless.

Then came signs of waking up. The winds arose gradually, becoming more and more intense, with dashes of rain. Then a tornado swept through villages and jungles, accompanied by terrific lightning and thunder. Nature is wide awake now, and has begun work with a haste and energy that seem intended to atone for the long idleness.

The life currents have started to flow again. Already the steady rains are falling, and for weeks and weeks they will fall; soaking everything, flooding the lowland districts, and bringing out everywhere an incredibly varied and luxuriant vegetation.

Then months hence there will come a rift in the clouds, the sun will peep through upon the water-soaked earth and teeming vegetation, and the work of undoing will begin.

But this is anticipation.

The rainy season is on now in earnest. The rice farms need no attention at present, and other occupations are hindered by the rains. Nature is also shaping the destiny of her children.

These simple Temne people, freed in a measure from the requirements of their ordinary occupations, respond the more readily to impulses that arise from social and intellectual instincts.

Led by the dumb craving of their natures, they have set an evening for a social gathering at the home of Sobah. The chief attraction, as everybody knows, will be story-telling, but there is to be no stiff formality. Everything will be spontaneous, and subject to the inspiration of the moment.

As the appointed evening comes on, the clouds thicken, and the rain has become a downpour. But what does that matter? There is little danger of injuring clothing,—if such an article is in evidence, and as to discomfort,—well, the street at this moment is full of youngsters who revel in the mud and water as if that were the acme of earthly bliss.

The older people are following an impulse only a little higher, as they stalk, heedless of rain, to Sobah's hut. A good fire is burning in the middle of the room, for the night will be dark and chill. With many a "How do", many a "Tankee" and many a touching of the inside fingertips, in conventional hand-shake, the greetings of the hour are passed. Oleemah has brought with him Soree, his kinsman from a distant village. Soree and Sobah are old acquaintances and warm friends, and not having seen each other for months are effusive in their greetings.

With many grunts and exclamations of pleasure they rush at each other and, swinging the outstretched arm in a semicircle, smite the open palms together in heartiest good-fellowship.

"Eh, fren, how do, I gladee fo' see yo' fo' true, true," said Sobah warmly. "How yo' kin 'tan'?"

"I well, tankee," answered Soree, with deep satisfaction, "en I gladee too much fo' come tell yo' how do. Yo' look lek say de ress bin plenty since de las' tem we bin meet up; yo' get skin big pass (surpass) me yown."

Each member of the company was allowed to seat himself as best he could, on the mud bed, on the floor, on anything. There was no need for haste, no record of time was kept.

Soree, as the guest from abroad, was questioned eagerly for news of his country and people, particularly of the war-boys, and he in turn was quite as interested in the gossip of the village.

Sobah had just related an incident from one of his trading expeditions, in which he had been imposed upon as to the quality of the articles bargained for, and in conclusion summed up his observation of human nature in the proverb: "Fis'erman nebber say he fish rotten."

After Sobah's bit of reminiscence, there was a silence broken only by the noise of the children, who were amusing themselves in their own peculiar way. An atmosphere of ease and endless leisure enveloped the place.

Finally an inspiration came to Mammy Yamah, who was “picking” cotton, and she said:

“One man bin deh (there), since w’en he born tay to-day, he hair white. Yo’ sabbee (know) dat?” The conundrum was familiar and easy, and one of the smaller boys, who happened to be listening, answered at once: “Cotton”.

There was a general stir among the pickaninnies, for here was something within their mental grasp, and they left the dog to sleep undisturbed, and ceased to play with the tame little ground-squirrel which Gengah had brought, partly to exhibit to the other children, but chiefly because he and the squirrel had become boon companions. The minds were all intent as Soree propounded this riddle:

“One ole man he inside ho’se, but he bear’-bear’ (beard) come out nah do’ (door).”

There was a puzzled silence until Oleemah, who sat nearest the door, and whose eyes were filled with the smoke that sought exit from the smouldering fire, started up with kindling face and exclaimed: “Eh, hey! Ladder wey (which) pusson no duh klim.”

This second conundrum, familiar to some present, and requiring the same word for solution as the preceding, was uttered in so triumphant a tone that a chorus of voices called out the double reply: “Smoke,” and the few who were less rapid in thought echoed the word with equal gusto.

Now came Mammy Mamenah with the following:

“De king he get ho’se, do’-mout’ (door-mouth) no deh, windah no deh, but pusson duh talk inside.”

This no one could guess, and Mammy was obliged to point to

a hen sitting on a nest at one end of the mud bed and say wisely: "Dat pusson duh sabbee; one week tem he go hearee de talk."

The patient brooder looked around as if to corroborate the woman's testimony, and as if thinking of the baby peeps that would announce her long vigil ended, and more active work begun.

This broad hint made the solution of the conundrum easy for most of the company, but Dogbah was still in the dark, as no one had named the answer specifically. Finally, unwilling to relinquish the point, although he was sure to bring ridicule upon himself, he asked: "Well, wey t'ing dat?"[50]

"Yo' stupid too much," replied Oleemah sarcastically. "Yo' no know dat egg no get do'-mout', no get windah, but pusson duh talk inside?"

Of course there was a loud laugh at Dogbah's expense, but he could console himself with knowing the solution of a very good conundrum.

Another pause followed, and then a young man who had spent several months in Freetown, had this to propose:

"Dey sew dress fo' one girl; he no deh, but w'en he reach, de dress jus' fit um."

Many laughable guesses were made, and occasioned no end of merriment. After the vain efforts ceased to amuse, the propounder explained that the dress was a fish-net. When once the comparison was clear, it was highly appreciated.

Gratified by the prestige his knowledge of town customs gave, the young man propounded another conundrum that proved almost as puzzling as his first one. It was this:

"One big ho'se bin deh, he get one post, no mo' (more)."

The problem seemed easy enough, but its solution proved to be a very difficult matter. Every conceivable likeness to a house with one post was offered, but still the Freetown sojourner showed his white teeth in a broad grin, and shook his head.

Konah had been taking lively interest in all the guessing, but thus far had not been able to give any correct answer except the ones already familiar to her. This time her active wits were working with unusual rapidity. The important part of a native house is the roof. Many of the farm-houses, Konah knew, consisted entirely of a thatch supported by posts. A short time before, she had seen the chief on a state occasion, beneath a large white cotton shelter with gay stripes, and—presto! she had the answer, for that house had but a single post. "Umbrella," she answered triumphantly, but still there was a look of perplexity on most of the faces, for the country article was made of bamboo, and was worn upon the head like a hat. However, as soon as reference was made to the one which the chief had, the matter was plain, and the conundrum was recognized as a good one to try on the uninstructed at the first opportunity.

Mammy Mamenah was making a mat out of palm fibre variously colored, but her mind had been as active as her fingers, and now she held the interest riveted upon her by:

"One man get t'ree slave; ef one gone, two no able fo' work."

The three fire-stones for the support of the rice-pot were not far off, and the sight of them suggested the solution to another woman, who then, reminded of her afternoon's task of broom-making, said:

"One man get plenty slave, he tie dem 'pon one rope, he hang dem up."

The children had all been used to gathering coarse, stiff grass, arranging it symmetrically, and tying it at the larger end, to form a broom, so they felt that the mental gymnastics had reached a point where they could participate. They had curled up in one corner of the room, to avoid the sharp tones, and the cuffs on the head that would follow if they disturbed their elders. Over the spot where they sat, the thatch was performing an expected part of its function, leaking, and perhaps the falling drops suggested: "Water hang."

The adults were slow in answering, but the shining black Foday very proudly responded, "Dat nar orange."

"Water 'tan' up, water grow," suggested by the previous answer, and propounded by Konah, was at once declared to be sugar-cane; for while the conundrums were new to some, they were current, and many knew their solutions.

"Two man bin close togedder, but dey nebber see each odder," was offered by the young man from Freetown, who thought that he was giving these rustics another puzzle, but he was much chagrined when "Two yi," came in a lusty chorus from the boys' corner, followed by a shout of derisive laughter. The answer "Two yi," suggested the next conundrum: "Two man wid ribber middle dem," and likewise suggested the response: "Two yi en nose," which came promptly.

"Me daddy buil' ho'se, soso (entirely) windah," was a good description of a fish-net which they had this very day seen woven by a man in the barri,[51] and consequently the answer was not long delayed.

"One t'ing, yo' walk 'pon um, but he nebber move." There was a moment of thought, broken by Konah's words: "Dat nar de groun'; but ef we tell Chameleon he no go believe we, because he t'ink say he one big pusson, he able fo' bus' de groun', broke um; dat make he duh mas' (tread) um soffle w'en he walker. Chameleon, wey leelee so!"

Sobah now introduced a slight change in the mental bill of fare.

"Hill," he announced, when there was a pause in the talk that threatened to be prolonged.

The interest of the company had begun to lag, but was quickened at once by this announcement. A hill requires effort in the ascent, and the term as used by Sobah was readily understood to signify a short story presenting a mental problem for solution, and leaving the question open for the hearers to exercise their ingenuity, and was a sort of challenge to find the solution.

"How?" was shouted back by the listeners, demanding to have the story with its proposition stated.

## The Three Twins.

"Hill!"

"How?"

"T'ree twin bin deh, two boy en one girl. One day den two boy go huntin', but de place wey dey go huntin' bin hilly place, so den lef' behine de hill. One twin look t'rou' de hill, en see one hog behine de hill; so he shoot t'rou' de hill, en de shot kill de hog. De odder twin he go t'rou' de place wey de big shot go, en he take de hog en kare um go home. W'en dey reach nah ho'se, den meet den sister done finis' cook de heart of de hog, de liver en de lung, befo' den reach home wid de hog.

The Three Twins.

"Now *yo'* fo' talk which one of dese t'ree twin do de big t'ing pass (surpass) all."

A lively argument followed this story, and it was evident that there was a difference of opinion. However, the majority seemed to think "de girl do de big t'ing pass all."

## Which Twin Restored His Father To Life?

Soree, between whom and Sobah was springing up a good-natured rivalry, now offered a twin story that was one better—in number at least—than Sobah's.

"Hill!" he announced.

"How?" was the response.

This indicates that all were ready to listen, so Soree related the following:

"Dis man heah he get four son, dey all twin. De fadder bin huntin' man. W'en he (his) pickin (pickaninnies) leelee he go huntin'; since dat he no come back. De wef he (her) heart trouble um, because he no know wey t'ing become of he man. W'en den four boy no done full grown, dey sized boy no mo' (merely), dey ax dem mammy 'bout dem daddy en de mammy answer: 'He bin go huntin'; me no know wey t'ing bin come of um.'

Which twin restored his father to life?

"So de las' boy, de one wey (who) make four, he say: 'I go surely know wey t'ing become of me faddah, I mus' fine um.'

"De odder one say: 'Ef yo' fine um, I kin manage fo' make faddah; ef yo' pick (collect) all de bone I kin join um.' De odder one say 'I kin gie body'; de odder one say: 'I go gie um life.' But dey no tell de mudder w'en dey duh talk 'bout dis t'ing, dey jus' ax um which road den daddy bin take w'en he wan' fo' go hunt. De mammy say: 'Dis back road.'

"Dem four boy dey grap (get up), dey go. Well, dey cut de way t'rough de bush, dey wandah, dey wandah far 'way nah de bush. De las' one he see one leelee road, he hole um wid all heen bruddah, he 'tan' up befo'. W'en dey go, dey go, dey go, dey meet one ribber. Jus' dey reach deh de las' one see heen fadder gun, en he meet heen dry head (skull). Now de odder t'ree boy jus' duh come, en de las' one tell um say: 'I finis' me yown part.'

"Well, de one wey bin say he go join de bone, he dibe bottom de wattah, he meet all dem bone, he bring um all 'pon top de lan', join dem all lek pusson, en he say: 'Look, me finis' me yown part.'

"De odder one he mix mud, he plaster um 'pon all de body, make de hair all. He take palm-leaf, he duck um inside de puttah-put,[52] he fash'n, fash'n um 'pon de mud. De blackness he duh shine, he fine de man. W'en he finis' he tell de odder twin, he say; 'Me done me yown part.'

"De one wey pass all fo' ole (old), he get one leelee horn wey kin protec' de life, kin bring life back. One country-fashion man make de horn, but not fo' dis purpose, he make um w'en de four twin leelee, fo' protec' dem, so nobody no go kill de baby. So dis boy go to de fadder to he nose, he put de horn deh, he blow inside de horn. De fadder sneeze, he grap, he take heen gun, he go home. Heen wef bin cry, he t'ink say somet'ing happen to heen pickin, dey all done die, because since early mornin' dey bin go 'way tay late nah evenin'. Jus' he look he see he man come nah road. De cry turn to laugh, great joy.

"Well, now dem four boy yeah, which one make dem get fadder?"

Soree allowed the argument to run on for a time, and noticing with deep satisfaction that opinions were hopelessly divided, closed the matter by saying with a touch of triumph in his tone: 'Nar dis de question dey duh argue tay (till) to-day. Yo' no able um.'

Sobah felt that his first story had not won him as much credit as he deserved, and so was constrained to offer another.

## Which One Was Most Greedy?

"T'ree man bin deh. Dey go far up country wey dey nar 'tranger to de king en de people. Dey all t'ree greedy too much, en because 'Tuckmah' mean say greedy pusson, pusson wey get sweet-mout', dis make all man duh call de one Tuckmahkodinay, de odder Tuckmahfongkah, en de las' one Tuckmahtontoun. W'en dey reach net tem to one big town, den go to de king heen (his) ho'se. Dey tell de king 'How do?' dey say: 'We nar 'tranger, we duh come out far country, make we sit down dis net to yo' town.'

"De king ax um plenty question: which side dey come out; how de ress 'tan', ef he plenty; ef dey bin see war boy w'en dey pass. Dey tell de king all t'ing wey dey bin see, en he gladee fo' de word wey dey talk; he gie dem one cow. Fo' few day dey sit down to dis king him town. Soon one mawnin' dey dribe de cow befo', dey walker tay dey reach to one leelee fa'm-ho'se; nobody no deh. Tuckmahkodinay he say: 'Make we kill de cow, make we yeat um.'

Dey go inside ho'se, dey fine cutlass, en calabas', en pot, en all t'ing fo' cook, but pusson no deh. One man take de cutlass fo' cut de cow he t'roat, fo' kill um. Tuckmahkodinay say: 'Bimeby de blood go was', I go hang me mout' underneat', make me ketch de blood.'

"De one wey hole de cutlass mistake, he cut off he cumpin (companion) him (his) head. He sorry, but wey t'ing fo' do? Nar (there are) de two man lef'. Dey cook de beef all. W'en dey finis' cook Tuckmahtontoun tell Tuckmahfongkah, he say: 'Go get wattah, make we yeat.'

"Deep well bin deh, he no far off, so Tuckmahfongkah say: 'Bimeby Tuckmahtontoun go yeat all de beef w'en I turn me back, make I mus' walk wid me back' (backwards).

"So he duh do, but befo' he kin t'ink say he reach to de well, he fa' over inside, he die. Tuckmahtontoun he see say he cumpin no come back, he say: 'Wey t'ing do Tuckmahfongkah, he no duh make hase come wid de wattah, make we yeat. I t'ink I betty go mese'f.' He go, he meet Tuckmahfongkah done die. Hese'f de one man lef'. He take de calabas', he full um, he hase (raise) um put um 'pon he head, he turn back come agin to wey he done cook. Befo' he reach close he see Fileentambo (Gazelle), he holler: 'Oh yah! Dah beef duh t'ief me sweet yeat (meat) wey I done cook. Ah, m-o-nay! I duh get trouble to-day.'

Tuckmahfongkah fals down the well.

"He put down de wattah, he run, he call: 'Hah, hah!'

"Jus' de beef hearee dis he turn quick, he see de man, he scare; he wan' fo' run, he foot slip, go inside de boilin' pot. He pull um quick, he run, he run. De man say de beef done kare all de sweetness, he greedy um de leelee bit wey he kare 'pon he foot, so he run aftah um, he run, sotay (till) he ketch um. W'en he wan' fo' lick de Fileentambo heen foot, dah foot wey bin inside de pot, Fileentambo he kick de man, bus' (burst) he t'roat. Tuckmahtontoun fa' down one tem, he die.

"Dem t'ree pusson deh, which one get sweet-mout' pass? Oonah (you) fo' judge."

Sobah was satisfied that his hill was a difficult one to climb; and, without waiting to hear the opinions that might be advanced, he turned his attention to replenishing the fire which had burned low.

The rain continued steadily outside, and a generous share of it found its way through the thatch. Darkness, thick and impenetrable, enveloped the hut. Inside, the fire, now blazing afresh, lit up the dusky faces and cast weird shadows upon the blackened mud walls. The air was thick with smoke and reeking with odors, but no one heeded that. These were big, overgrown children, bent on an entire night's amusement and entertainment in the most refined form they knew; and, like all children, they must enjoy their game in spite of discomforts, perhaps even enjoy it the more because of the discomforts.

Soree felt that he was expected to furnish the next story, but some delicate inner sense told him that they had had enough mental nuts to crack, and so he considerately turned to stories of a more fanciful and entertaining type.

"Yo' know dah story 'bout Mr. Spider en Mr. Lepped?" he asked to gain time to collect his thoughts. They had heard similar stories, but were just as eager to hear this one. After scratching his head thoughtfully a few minutes, Soree cleared his throat as a signal that he was ready to begin.

## Mr. Spider Creates A Frightful Tornado.

"Now Spider, he en Lepped bin fren' one tem; dey sit down togedder (live) to one ole fa'm-ho'se. W'en dey go hunt, dey no see any beef. *So* dey do tay till hangry ketch um *bad*. Now Lepped say: 'Come go, Spider, come make we go yeat we (our) pickaninny.'

Mr. Spider creates a frightful tornado

"Spider say: 'Yes, nar true, but make we yeat yo' yown fus', because yo' fus' talk.' Lepped 'gree. Bimeby dey done yeat Lepped he pickin all, en him wef; but not to one day dey yeat all. One day dey kill one, odder day dey kill one tay (till) all finis'. Turn done come fo' yeat Spider yown. Spider say: 'To-morrow make we meet to one odder fa'm-ho'se, bottom one big 'tick (tree) yondah.'

"Lepped say: 'All ret.'

"Now Spider lef Lepped, he go home, he go cut plenty long palm-branch, big long palm-branch. He tie um, make big bunch. He shabe (divide) de bunch one one to he (his) pickin en he (his) wef. Well, Spider go mawnin' to de place, he meet Lepped deh. All two duh sit down talk. Dey hearee noise. Spider heen wef Nahker en de pickin duh drag dem palm leaf 'pon de groun' fo' make Lepped t'ink say tornado go come. W'en Spider en Lepped hearee dis yeah big noise, Spider grap (get up), he knock he foot 'pon de groun', he say:

"'Mr. Lepped, yo' able fo' sit down? Big breeze duh come, he go sweep we 'way. De place wey he go lef we, now deh we go die, we no go see none o' we famble agin.' He say: 'Mr. Lepped, do fren' tie me quick, befo' dis breeze yeah reach. Make he no kare me go.'

"Lepped say: 'No;' he say: 'Fren', yo' fus' tie me.'

"Spider say: 'No, fren', yo' fus' tie me.'

"Lepped say: 'No, yo' fus'.'

"Spider get up, he say: 'Well, I 'gree, because dis storm heah wan' big, big people, he go kare yo' up fus' ef I no tie yo'.'

"He kare um to dah big plum tree, he say: ''Tan' up 'traight, no shake, 'tan' up soffle.'

"Lepped he 'tan' up close de 'tick. Spider go cut rope. Long tem Spider bin huntin' fo' flog Lepped, but he no able um, so now he pull dis cunnie. All dis tem dey hearee de breeze duh come. Lepped say: 'Make hase, de breeze duh come.'

"Spider bring de rope, he begin fo' tie Lepped f'om he toe 'roun' de 'tick, tay he reach to he neck, 'roun', 'roun', 'roun' de 'tick. W'en he finis' Lepped no kin move, he no able fo' shake he body. Spider laugh, he say: 'I bin do yo' fool.' He tell he pickin, he say: 'Me pickin, oonah (you) hebe de whip, oonah (you) come, we done ketch de brah (brother).'

"Him pickin dey klim 'pon de 'tick, dey yeat de plum, dey hebe (throw) de seed 'pon Lepped he head. Aftah dey done yeat dey come down, dey begin conk (strike) Mr. Lepped, dey *conk* um, dey say: 'Yo' nar (are) dog, yo' kin yeat people. Come yeat we of yo' able.'

"Lepped look dem wid bad yi, but he no know how fo' do.

"Spider tell Lepped, say: 'Aintee (is it not) so any day yo' kin hole me, yo' flog me?' Now he go broke whip, he say: 'Mese'f I go flog yo' to-day.'

"Spider bring de whip come, he flog Lepped, he flog um, he flog um. Lepped he say: 'Do yah!' He beg long, long tem. Spider no 'gree, he flog um sotay (till) he tire, den he go home."

Loud laughter and explosive ejaculations followed the close of the story, and showed how thoroughly Spider's successful trick was appreciated. Soree himself laughed heartily, and added: "Spider he smart man fo' true, true. Nobody nebber go ketch up wid Spider."

This last remark was directed at Sobah; and he, taking it as a challenge, proceeded to relate a story in which matters were somewhat evened up between Leopard and Spider.

## Mr. Leopard Shows His Hand.

As if to make the retribution appear in the light of poetic justice, Sobah devised a connecting link between this story and the one just told.

Mr. Leopard shows his hand.

"W'en dey reach home," he said, referring to the time Spider flogged Leopard so unmercifully, "Spider go cut one big calabas' (gourd), he dig one leelee hole inside um, nuff fo' hese'f to pass. He put um deh to de co'ner of he ho'se.

"Well, w'en one week done pass, dem bug-a-bug (white ants) dey come yeat all dem rope, en Lepped go home. He no get 'trenk because he no bin yeat anyt'ing fo' one week. He go try sotay (till) he ketch leelee beef, befo' he get 'trenk fo' ketch big beef. De day wey make t'ree, he get leelee 'trenk, he hole de road, he walker slow, slow, fo' go to Spider heen ho'se.

"Nahker he duh cook. Den all hearee step. One leelee pickin, wid name Kokany, wey (which) mean go watch, he go look, he say: 'Mammy, 'tranger duh come; hide de ress (rice) nah bottom bed.'

"Nahker come out, he peep, he say: 'Spider, we die to-day, Lepped duh come.'

"Spider call he pickin, he say: 'Ef yo' lef' behine, en yo' get big trouble, de fault to oonah (you).'

"Dey all duh follow um, go inside de gourd wey (which) 'tan' up nah de co'ner de ho'se. De place wey dey pass go inside bin up. W'en dey all done go inside, Spider roll de t'ing over, de mout' he nah de groun'.'

"Lepped come, he meet big pot ress 'tan' up nah de fiah, en one big pot soup 'tan' up 'pon de groun'. De beef wey dey cook, nar bush-hog. Den t'ing all done ready was' fo' take up de yeat. Lepped he sit down, he laugh fus'. Now he take up all dah ress, he take dah soup, he turn dah soup all 'pon de ress, he yeat *all*, he no lef one grain. Spider wan' cry, he deh inside dah hole."

This was more than Dogbah could stand. "No talk mo'," he cried impulsively, "Yo' make mese'f wan' cry fo' yeat dah ress en dah bush-hog," and he drew in a long breath that seemed to typify the longing of his soul.

"Ah! Yo greedy (begrudge) pusson too much," Sobah answered sternly, but deigned no further reply.

"Well, aftah Lepped done yeat, he go outside de fa'm-ho'se, he smell all 'roun', but he no smell Spider. He go inside, he come smell smell. He look, he bootoo (stooped over), he peep, he see one leelee gourd yandah, he go smell deh, he smell ole Mr. Spider. He take he foot, he krape de gourd, he turn um over. All de spider dey scatter, dey so plenty he no know which one fo' ketch. All go f'om um, dey all go inside bush yandah. Bottom one big tree dey go sit down. W'en Lepped bin yeat dah beef, he hebe (throw) de bone nah groun'. W'en Spider duh run go, he kare one leelee ole bone wey Lepped t'row 'way. He hole de bone, he sit bottom one big 'tick, he en he wef en he pickin. Den come Mr. Lepped, he take swing (sling), he put stone deh, he twis' um 'roun', he sen' um, he knock Bucknaykuhnunt, de mos' large pickin. De pickin say: 'W-a-y-ee!'

"Spider say: 'Ah! No holler! Shut mout' one tem. Bimeby Lepped go come ketch we. Take dah bone, make yo' suck um.'

"De pickin no talk, he take de bone, he hole um, but he no suck um, he too sick fo' suck um. Lepped sen' odder stone, he knock odder pickin. So he duh do tay he knock de pickin all. Now de same word Spider duh tell ebery tem to de pickin, but de bone he *one* no mo'. W'en stone knock one of he pickin, Spider take de bone f'om de fus', he gie to de odder one wey las' get de trouble. Now Lepped sen' one stone, he size pass (beyond) de fus', he sen' um go knock he wef Nahker nah jaw-bone. He wef say: 'W-y-ee! Me mammy to-day.' (He mean say he mammy kin feel fo' um pass odder pusson, he wan' see um).

"Spider say: 'Oh, wef! lef' fo' holler, shut mout' one tem. Bimeby Lepped go ketch we. Take de bone, make yo' suck um.'

"At las' Mr. Lepped take stone big lek dis town, put um inside de swing. He sen' um go knock Mr. Spider nah he forehead. Spider cry: 'W-a-y-ee! Trouble, trouble! Me mammy to-day!'

"He wef say: 'Ah! Spider, lef fo' holler, shut mout' one tem, bimeby Lepped go ketch we. Look de bone fo' suck."

"Spider say: 'Yo' craze? Aftah pusson knock yo' cumpin (companion) yo' no tell um hush-yah?[53] Yo' say make yo' come suck bone. Nar tem dis fo' suck bone?'

"Spider holler tay Lepped come ketch dem. Now he flog dem all. Nahker en de pickin dey die, but Spider run go odder country.

"Pusson nebber kill Spider w'en dey flog um; dey make he go so he kin feel pain, so he kin 'member wey t'ing he do.

"Tay to-day, Spider he en Lepped no to fren' agin."

So matters were equalized, and justice satisfied, but the story-tellers were not willing to let Mr. Leopard off.

Gondomah's face showed that he was repressing a desire to speak, and, noticing this, Sobah condescendingly urged him to proceed.

Thus encouraged Gondomah began, rather timidly at first, to recount the ruse of Mr. Leopard by which he secured food in time of famine.

## Mr. Leopard Fools The Other Animals.

"Now two animal get dis play, dah Lepped en all dem beef. All dem beef bin meet up fo' make play one evenin' tem w'en dem moon duh shine. Dey gadder 'roun de place, dey tie fench, dey buil' leelee ho'se inside de fench. De nex' evenin' tem dey play, dey beat de drum, dey dance all. Now ole Mr. Lepped, hangry duh ketch um, so he come do cunnie. Because he wan' fo' ketch dem beef fo' make he yeat dem, he lay down, he lay down flat; he no die, he do cunnie, he shut he yi, he make altogedder lek die.

"One of Lepped he pickin he come out play. W'en he run inside ho'se he look heen daddy, he 'fraid fo' true, he come close um leelee bit, he ax um, say:

"'Daddy, wey t'ing do yo'?'

Mr. Leopard fools the other animals.

"He no get answer; he pull one big cry, he run tell de odder pickin say:

"'Eh! M-o-nay! We daddy done die, we no get daddy to-day.'

"Dey all duh cry, duh cry; dey run wid cry to all dem beef fo' say:

"'We daddy done die, make yo' mus' come cry fo' um.'

"Well, all dem beef dey come 'roun' um, dey sorry, dey gadder fo' cry fo' Lepped wey (which) die. Dey begin fo' make noise, dey cry lek fo' die pusson. Fus' Cunnie Rabbit come, he look Lepped, he look um long tem, he say:

"'Dis yeah beef he no die, he jus' duh do cunnie.'

"So he grap (get up), he go sit down yandah fo' run one tem, he say:

"'Die pusson nebber blow (breathe).'

"Well, Lepped jus' duh blow leelee, leelee, w'en dem beef no take notice.

"W'en Cunnie Rabbit say die pusson nebber blow, dem beef say:

"'Cunnie Rabbit, yo' nar fool!'

"He answer um, say: 'All ret, I fool.'

"Den he go sit down to de las' part yandah, so he kin fus' run go w'en Lepped go grap (get up) fo' ketch dem beef. Well, dem beef wey say Cunnie Rabbit fool, dey come sit down close Lepped, dey all duh cry, duh cry.

"Bimeby Lepped grap fo' ketch, en all dem beef wey bin hearee wey Cunnie Rabbit talk, dey all run.

"Well, dem beef wey say Cunnie Rabbit fool, Lepped ketch um all.

"'Pon dem beef Lepped en he pickin lib tay (till) hangry tem done."

Gondomah gained confidence as the story proceeded, and was soon speaking with a freedom and earnestness that would have done even Sobah credit. Mr. Leopard had found a new champion, and was growing in favor with an emotional audience, that was ready to applaud any form of cunning that proved successful. Konah, however, was much gratified to note that "Cunnie Rabbit" had not been deceived.

## A Case Of "Tit For Tat."

In the interval that followed Gondomah's story, a little diversion occurred. Two of the boys had been tantalizing each other, and matters had reached such a pitch that one spoke slightingly of the other's "daddy," and the other retorted by making a loud sucking noise through his teeth, an insult no Temne lad would allow to go unpunished, therefore a fight ensued.

"Yo' curse me daddy, I conk (strike) yo'," and the blow came promptly.

A case of Tit for Tat.

"Yo' suck teet' 'pon me?" and the counter blow was equally

prompt. The battle promised to be prolonged to an extent that would interfere with the story-telling, so a man near by sent the boys flying to opposite corners of the room.

When quiet reigned once more, Sobah began the story he was preparing to relate when the fight started.

"Now Spider he get he village, but he no sleep deh, he sleep nah he fa'm-ho'se. One day he go set trap, he ketch dah Lepped he pickin (pickaninny), en he come yeat um. De Lepped no bin deh w'en Spider kare de pickin go. W'en Lepped come, he cry nah de bush fo' he pickin. Now de same tem, Spider call he cumpin (companion), 'Come go play, come go play.' W'en de Lepped hearee um he lef fo' cry, he silence, he come close de fa'm-ho'se. De Spider no know Lepped deh, he jus' duh talk, say: 'We yeat fine t'ing, to-day, de t'ing mark, mark. He favor dah pusson wey duh cry nah bush yandah; dah pusson heen pickin we yeat.'

"De Lepped done hearee um, but Spider no know. He duh talk tay de t'ing come close um. Jus' he see um he run, he go inside de fa'm-ho'se, he de only one deh inside. Now he make fiah, he take dem pot, dem kettle, en all dem t'ing wey (which) pusson get inside ho'se, dem t'ing wey duh soun'. He beat dem all fo' make big noise: he holler fo' make de Lepped go say: 'Dey *plenty* inside de fa'm-ho'se. Now Spider heen wef en heen t'ree pickin come open de do' fo' come inside. Dis de tem de Lepped follow come inside. W'en 'fraid ketch Spider en he famble dey all klim, dey lef' de Lepped sit down nah groun'. W'en he done 'tay leelee bit, one pickin wey (who) pass dem all fo' young, he say he done tire fo' hang. Now de daddy say: 'Fa' down make Lepped yeat yo'.'

"Now he fa' down, en de Lepped yeat um.

"Now de nex' one say, hese'f done tire.

"Daddy Spider say: 'Fa' down, now,' en he fa' down, en de Lepped yeat um.

"Now de odder pickin say he done tire, but dah pickin ole pass de odder two, he 'trong leelee bit; dah make Spider say: 'Change yo' han'.'

"Now he change he han' fo' some tem, den he say: 'I done tire,' en he fa' down, en Lepped yeat um.

"At las' de wef Nahker, he say he done tire, en Spider say: 'Yo' wey big so? Fa' down, now, yo' go get de trouble.'

"Nahker fa' down, Lepped yeat um. Spider he one lef' hang. W'en he done tire he take leelee condah (bark) wey bin deh 'pon dah 'tick wey Spider hang, he hebe (throw) um to dah Lepped down. Now de Lepped grip de condah, he mean say he hole Spider. W'en he duh fet wid de condah (bark) Spider come down soffle, he run, he go hide. Pusson nebber able ketch Spider, because he cunnie."

Mr. Spider's ability to get himself out of the most serious difficulty, was fast bringing him back to the position of popular favorite. It was not at all to his discredit that he did not risk his life to save his wife and children. Soree, who had been biding his time, seized the favorable opportunity to complete the supremacy of Mr. Spider, and without preliminaries plunged into his story.

## Dr. Spider's Fatal Prescriptions.

"One tem Lepped get t'ree pickin, en heen pickin dey sick, so he duh walker all 'roun' de country fo' look fo' doctah. Den Spider grap (get up), he tell Lepped say, he say: 'Now me one big, big doctah. Ef yo' gie me yo' pickin, I go make dem all well.'

Dr. Spider's fatal prescriptions.

"So Lepped call de pickin, en he gie um to Spider wid fine present. Spider take de pickin, en he kare um inside one fench wey he build, fo' doctah um. He tell Lepped say, he say: 'Make nobody no come inside heah, en yo'se'f no mus' come inside heah.'

"So Spider dig one long hole f'om he yown home to dah place wey he duh doctah dem pickin. W'en he done kare dem pickin inside, he run t'rou' dis hole, en he go to heen ho'se. He call he yown pickin, he say, make dem bring pot, en ress, en palm-ile, en salt, en peppy. So w'en heen pickin done bring all dis, Spider grip Lepped heen pickin, en he kill dem. He make de pickin cook plenty ress, en he yeat dem all, he en him pickin, but he tell him pickin, make dem no yeat dem bone.

"So aftah one moon, Spider go out to Lepped, he say: 'I ready fo' pull yo' pickin now, dey done well. But w'en I duh pull dem pickin, I go tie rope 'pon dem, make yo'se'f draw dem out.'

"So Spider hese'f he go pass t'rou' dis hole heah, he go nah he yown home. Den he gie signal to Lepped fo' make he draw he pickin out; but w'en Lepped draw, he see soso (merely) bone, en he fa' down yandah fo' cry.

"W'en do' clean, Lepped take hese'f, he put hese'f inside one hamper, en he put coal[54] 'pon hese'f, en he call heen servant, en he tell heen servant, say: 'Tie me good fashion wid dis cord, en kare me to Spider, en tell um, say: 'Now me sen' coal fo' um,' fo' Spider was a blacksmit' at dis tem now.

"So heen servant take de hamper, en he kare um go to Spider, en he tell um say: 'Daddy Lepped say: "Make I bring dis coal fo' yo'."'

"But Spider look de coal, he see Lepped lay down bottom, he tell he servant say: 'All ret.'

"So Spider take one iron, he put um nah fiah, en de iron red hot. He say: 'Make I try dis coal, ef now good coal dis.'

"So he take dis iron, en he chook um t'rou' dis hamper. Den Lepped holler, en he kill Lepped deh, en make big dinnah fo' hese'f en he pickin."

There was again a note of triumph in Soree's voice as he recited these tragic events, for certainly as Mr. Leopard had been disposed of, Sobah could not produce him alive again in order to make another story.

It was far past midnight, and there were signs of weariness on the part of the younger members, but there was no thought of breaking up the gathering. In fact they had been enjoying themselves so genuinely, that they were scarcely aware of the passage of time.

Sobah arose, placed fresh wood on the fire, causing it to emit a heavy smoke; then squatting down again on the floor he began to relate another of Mr. Spider's many exploits.

## Mr. Spider "Pulls" A Supply Of Beef.

"De Frog he leelee beef. One tem he duh go walker. He meet one cow wey belong to de king. Well, dis cow, pusson kin kare um ebery mawnin' fo' go yeat, tie um nah one place (pasture). Well, ef yo' meet dis cow, en yo' say: 'Cow open!' he kin open he mout', he kin swallow yo'.

"Well, ebery mawnin' de Frog kin go wid leelee knef en bucket, he tell de cow: 'Open!' De cow kin open he mout', de Frog joomp inside, en de cow swallow um. De cow fat, en de Frog nebber hurt de cow w'en he cut dis plenty fat, but he no fo' cut one place, de heart; even ef de fat plenty deh, he no fo' cut um. Ef he cut um de cow fa' down de same place, he die. Aintee de life deh to de heart? Aftah de Frog done cut de fat, he come back to de mout', he say: 'Cow open!' De cow open he mout', de Frog come out, he go home, he cook. Aftah he finis' cook, he call Spider come yeat. Aftah dey done yeat, w'en Spider feel de sweetness, he say:

"'W-y-ee, fren'! Which side yo' go get dis beef yeah?'

Mr. Spider "pulls" a supply of beef.

"De Frog say: 'I bin go tell yo', but w'en yo' fine anyt'ing sweet fo' yeat, yo' nebber slack fo' go aftah de same t'ing. Yo' nebber say, "Make I wait," so ef I tell yo', yo' go kill pusson cow, en I no able de palaver. I know yo', yo' get big yi.'

"Spider say: 'No, fren', I no go do so.'

"Well, de Frog tell um say. 'All ret, mus' come to-morrow mawnin', early in de mawnin'.'

"Spider say: 'All ret.' He no sleep; middle de net he get up, he go to de Frog heen do', he say:

"'Brah, (Brother,) day done broke.'

"De frog come out, he say: 'No, day no broke, do' no clean; wait leelee bit mo'.'

"Spider go lay down fo' few minute, den he get up, he too eager. He go to de Frog heen do'-mout', he make noise lek fowl kin make w'en day wan' break: 'Kokooriko-o-o!' Den he knock. 'Kong, kong!' He say: 'Brah, day done broke.'

"De Frog say: 'Ah, no! Yo' see yo' yown trick; not yet.'

"Spider go fo' few minute, he come ag'in, he holler lek one bird. Day kin done begin fo' break, yo' see leelee clear befo' dis bird make noise: 'Dew, dew, dew, dew!'

"Spider say: 'Brah, day done broke.'

"De Frog come out, he say: 'Lef me! Now so yo' trick 'tan.' He say: 'Ef yo' humbug me again, I no go kare yo', I go me one (alone).'

"Well, Spider go lay down soffle tay (till) day done broke. Now de frog go call um. W'en Spider come he take he bly (basket), he follow de Frog. Dey jus' go tief de grease. Ef de king know, now great trouble come 'pon dem, dey no get permission fo' do dis t'ing. W'en dey done go inside, dey begin fo' cut.

"De Frog he tell Spider, he say: 'Yo' see dah place deh?'—he mean de heart—'I no care ef plenty rich palm-ile deh, no venture fo' cut deh. De minute yo' touch deh wid knef, de Cow go die.'

"Spider say: 'All ret.' Spider full heen bly, den Frog full heen bowl, dey go. But w'en dey wan' fo' come out, dey fo' say to de Cow: 'Open.' W'en dey reach home, de Frog tell Spider: 'To-morrow no come, make we slack fo' to-morrow.'

"Spider say: 'All ret'; he go home. He en he wef en he pickin dey cook all, dey yeat all.

"Well, aftah dey done yeat, Spider go, he plant (plait) plenty bly, two tem as big as de fus'. Mawnin' early he get up, he gie all heen pickin dem bly, he say: 'Come, oh, go.'

"De Frog bin tell um not to go to-morrow, but he no hearee; he go, he say: 'Cow open!' De Cow stupid, he open, he swallow Spider wid all heen pickin. Dey cut, dey full all de bly, dey go home, dey cook, dey yeat. Dis Frog he no know say Spider bin go deh. Ebery mawnin' now so Spider duh do. W'en dey cut de grease one day, de nex' mawnin' dey meet mo' come, but he nebber plenty lek de fus'. One tem Spider no kare none of heen pickin, he one, no mo', go. He see plenty big, big grease, big, big fat deh to de heart. He no believe de word Frog bin talk, he get too big yi. He cut de heart. Jus' he cut um de Cow fa' down one tem. Spider come, he say: 'Cow open.' Cow no able open, because he done die. Spider he no know how fo' do. Pusson come evenin' tem fo' de Cow. Den meet he done die, den 'plit um, dey call de pickin, den gie um de inside part fo' was'. Dey kare um nah wattah-side, dey was' de heart, de inside part all. Because Spider leelee, dey no see w'en he joomp 'pon top de bridge. He call, he tell de pickin, say:

"'Look how oonah (you) hebe (throw) dirty 'pon me w'en yo' duh was' deh.'

"Dem pickin begin fo' beg um, dey say: 'Daddy, do yah, do yah! No do we not'ing, we no know, we mistake.'

"Spider say: 'I no 'gree.'

"He go nah town to de king, he go lay dis complain'. W'en he done tell de king all how de pickin do um, de king cut de cow he foot, all de bigness of he foot,[55] he wan' gie um to Spider.

"Spider say: 'I no wan' dis foolish t'ing yeah.'

"Dem cut de han', dem lay um 'pon de foot. Spider no 'gree. Las' dey take de head, lay um 'pon top. Spider kin 'trong fo' yeat, he lazy fo' wuk. I no care ef anyt'ing fo' yeat how he big, he kin take um, but ef yo' gie um one grain ress fo' tote (carry), he no able um, he heaby. But how de yeat may big, ef *cow* yo' gie um, he go hase um go. Spider take all dis beef, he tote (carry) um go. W'en he reach middle de road, he see 'tranger duh come, he call quick fo' he'p. He 'krape de groun' leelee bit, he dig one hole, en he set de cow him head inside de hole; but he no put all, so dat ef pusson draw um, he no go be hard fo' pull um deh. He tie rope to de horn, en he do lek say he duh draw. So w'en he duh do dis, he see dah people duh come yandah wid plenty cow. W'en dey reach close um, he tell um, say:

"'Oonah come, oonah come quick! De king heen cow wan' fo' go inside hole.'

"He put heen han' 'pon de head, he do lek he duh draw, he say:

"'Come, he'p me; make we pull de king heen cow f'om dis hole.'

"So de 'tranger all come, dey begin fo' go take de rope, en w'en dey draw, de cow head bin lef' nah dem han'. Spider make lek he vex 'pon um, he say:

"'Yo, oh! Oonah done cut off de cow heen head. All ret, oonah take um, oonah bring odder cow. Ef de king hear jus' now dat oonah kill de cow (because nar de king life oonah take 'way so), de treatment oonah go get f'om de king, I no able fo' 'spress um.'

"Dis cow wey Spider done kill bin sacred cow, now he 'tan' fo' de life of de king. Ef anybody kill de cow, now de king life he cut off. Dey done pull sacrifice to dis cow.

"Dem 'tranger den 'fraid fo' true. Dey gie Spider one big cow, dey yown cow wey dey bin bring. Spider say:

"'Now dis one cow oonah gie fo' dis sacred cow? I no wan'.'

"Dem people no know how fo' do, den duh trimble wid fear. Now, dey take odder large cow, dey gie Spider all two; he refuse. He get big yi, he say he no wan', he jus' only wan' fo' go 'port dem to de king. Dem people beg, dey ketch odder cow agin, dey gie Spider de t'ree cow. He say: 'All ret, oonah go.'

"W'en dey done go, Spider take all heen plenty beef, he go. He done rich by heen cunnie."

Soree was trying hard to recall a suitable story to follow the one just ended, but at that very moment a fowl began to crow. "Dah fowl craze," exclaimed Oleemah, thinking it impossible that morning was at hand, and with that he arose and thrust his head out of the window.

"Nar true word dah fowl duh talk," he admitted, as he saw the first signs of approaching dawn. The clouds had thinned, the rain had almost ceased, and in consequence the dense darkness was breaking away.

Reminded by these signs that life is not all fiction, Oleemah turned to the door and strode away to his hut. His movements broke the spell that had so long held the company, and soon all had scattered to their several huts, feeling that the night had been well spent.

## CHAPTER IX

# AN AFTERNOON IN THE BARREH[56]

It was some weeks after the night gathering at Sobah's house. A man, the most skilful weaver in the village, was seated at his simple loom, which had been set up in the barreh, and was busily engaged weaving country cloth.

The rain had been but light recently, and this afternoon Nature seemed undecided whether to smile or to weep. Sunshine and shower engaged in playful rivalry, but each seemed equally pleased for the other to win. The air was conducive to idleness, and the barreh was an ideal spot for loafing. When Sobah reached the place he found a dozen men and women, and fully as many children, assembled. A few women brought work to busy their fingers, cotton to spin, and fish-nets to weave, but most were content to allow the hour to provide for itself.

Of course Konah was there, for her instinct told her that such a time and place would bring something worth hearing.

Sobah was seated in a hammock, and had unconsciously taken a position so that the others were grouped around him.

The situation was suggestive, and Oleemah, noticing it, requested a story. As he was warmly seconded by others, Sobah not unwillingly complied.

## The Dancing Bird.

"Well, I tell yo' story 'bout one man en one boy," he said after a little reflection. "Dis man bin huntin' man. One day he go huntin', en he ketch one fine beef, young beef, en he bring um home. Dis huntin' man he get plenty pickin. Ef he gie one boy de beef, all de odder go vex; so he gie dis beef to dem all, fo' make dem play wid um. De beef no die. Dey mine um[57] sotay (till) he begin use dem. Now one po' boy bin lib close to dis huntin' man heen ho'se. He en he mammy dey no get pusson fo' make fa'm fo' dem, en dis huntin' man heen pickin all, dey nebber 'gree fo' make dis po' boy play wid de beef wey dey get; en de man hese'f no 'gree. W'en dey go nah fa'm de po' boy take de beef, he play wid um all day. W'en de man en heen pickin wan' come home f'om de fa'm, he put um back. Nar so he duh do any day.

"One day, w'en he take dis beef, de beef he die nah he han'. He done 'fraid, he lef de beef, he run go home.

"Now dem people come back. W'en dey open de place, dey meet de beef done die.

"Now dey ax de boy, dey say: 'Who kill dis beef heah?'

"Fus' de boy no wan' fo' answer. Now dey begin fo' knock um, dey knock um tay (till) he say *he* kill de beef.

"Now de man say: 'Yo' mus' surely gie back odder beef fo' dis one wey yo' bin kill.'

"De boy beg *so-t-a-y*, but de man no 'gree. De boy take he cutlass, he go set trap. Any day he go, but not'ing no ketch. Any day w'en he come, de huntin' man *mus'* beat um fo' dat beef.

The Dancing Bird.

"Now de mammy beg, he beg good fashion, but de man no 'gree fo' lef de palaver, he say de pickin *mus'* gie um dah beef.

"De mammy say: 'Well, take me pickin one tem (at once), de t'ing yo' wan' fo' do, make yo' do um one tem, make I see.'

"Mawnin' de boy set trap, but all day he no ketch. He come home evenin' tem. W'en he come home he cry, he say: 'Because dey go come beat me.' Dem pusson dey come home. Sometem de boy bin go hide under he mammy bed. Nar so dey bin do any day, dey bin beat um any day. Now one day de boy cry, he come out under rain, he go set trap, en he ketch dis beef yeah. He gladee, he gladee bad, fo' wey he get um. Now he bring um, he gie um to dis bad man.

"One day de boy go walker, he go close one big, big wattah; de wattah 'roun'. Now he go meet dah fine, fine bird wey kin sing, kin dance. He 'tan' lek canary, but not to canary. Alligator bin deh inside de wattah. W'en dah boy see dah plenty bird over de wattah, he see dey duh dance, dey duh sing, he wan ketch one, make he sing fo' um. W'en he try fo' cross, now he fa' down nah de wattah, en alligator come yandah fo' yeat um. Now he swim, he make hase, en he cross; he go ketch one of dah bird heah. Now he cross over back, now he come home. W'en he reach to he ho'se, he put de bird down 'pon de flo'. De bird sing, he dance. Now plenty people come fo' look dis bird wey duh sing, weh duh dance. Ef anybody wan' look um, he bring one piece clot' sotay dis po' mammy rich. Anybody, dah chief, dah king, dey kin come look dis bird how he kin dance; dey bring present to dis boy. Dis boy keep dis bird inside bly (basket). Now he go to de fa'm wid he mammy. Well, dis bad huntin' man, he go pull dis pickin heen bird, he put um down inside de ho'se, en de bird begin fo' sing, he begin fo' dance. W'en de man see de boy duh come yandah, he take de bird back quick. De boy come say: 'Who bin pull dis bird heah?' De man nebber answer. Now de boy say: 'All ret,' en he lef fo' talk.

"Plenty people come, dey say dey come look dis bird wey kin dance. Dey bring plenty present fo' gie dis boy heah. Now he pull de bird, de bird dance, he sing. Dis ooman he rich, he get plenty. Now de pickin put de bird inside bly agin, en he go to de fa'm wid he mammy. De man pull de bird agin, he look um. W'en he put de bird down he dance leelee bit, den he say:

"'Ef yo' wan' make me dance fine, make yo' kare me nah yard. Dah dance wey I go dance, he go pass all fo' fine.'

"De man he t'ink say dis nar true. He take de bird, kare um go nah yard; he put um down; de bird fly go. He bin 'deed make dis man fool."

Both Sobah's tone and the drift of the story indicated that a rich climax was approaching, and many were shaking already with anticipated pleasure; so the story was interrupted here until the pent-up delight had been set free.

"Now de boy come home. W'en he go look inside de place, he no see de bird, he ax he mammy. He mammy say he no know. Now he ax de man, en dis one say he no know. Now one ole ooman say, 'Dah huntin' man take de bird,' he say. 'W'en dem people come fo' look de bird, he bin pull um, bin put um nah yard, en de bird fly, he go.'

"Now de boy go to de man, he say: 'I wan' me bird jus' now, to-day.'

"De man wan' talk de boy, but he say: 'No talk, I go burn yo' ho'se jus now.'

"De man he nebber sleep, he nebber sit down all day; he walker all day close de ribber, make trap fo' ketch bird. Now one day he fine de same wattah, wey de boy bin ketch dis bird. Now he see dem plenty bird wey duh sing, wey duh dance. W'en he wan' go ketch de bird he fa' down nah de wattah so, en alligator ketch um, he yeat um.

"Dat make he no good fo' do leelee pickin bad. Ef pusson do leelee pickin t'ing wey (which) bad, trouble go ketch um wey (which) go pass he yown."

Kindness towards children is not a part of the Temne social

code, generally, at least not a conscious part; but Sobah was the unconscious embodiment of many of the better characteristics of his people, and personal experience had made him more than usually considerate and gentle. So he felt that this story contained a serious message, and he was the chosen mouthpiece.

"Now dat bin true word," he added, looking reprovingly around the company. "Any pusson wey (who) do leelee pickin bad, trouble go ketch um wey (which) go pass him yown."

After repeating this impressive warning, Sobah sat long in deep reflection. He was recalling another story, wherein the would-be evil doer received a just retribution. As soon as he felt moved to speak, he began his tale.

## The Wicked Is Taken In His Own Snare.

"Dis 'tory 'bout one boy, he name Pass-all-king-fo'-wise. De boy heen (his) fadder bin king. Well, de fadder get so many wef dat he no bin notice w'en one wef bin loss f'om um, bin go hide nah (in) one fa'm-ho'se. He (she) lib heah tay (till) all he (her) mate (associate wives') pickin done grow big. Well, one day dese pickin yeah come, dey brush fa'm. It happen dey begin fo' brush near de same ole fa'm-ho'se wey (where) dis ooman duh hide. He (she) shame fo' see he mate pickin all done grow up big, en he yown pickin leelee no mo'. So he (she) run wid he pickin, come out agin f'om dis fa'm-ho'se, he go far 'way, he meet big bug-a-bug (ant) hill, he klim 'pon top, he sit down, he say:

"'Oh, I wis' me pickin done 'trong fo' brush lek dis one heah.'

The Wicked is taken in his own Snare.

"Now de bug-a-bug hill he talk to um, he say: 'Even ef yo' pickin no 'trong nuff fo' brush, I go gie um sense en riches all two.'

"So de ooman say, he say: 'All ret.'

"At once de ooman he see he baby he grow big man, he rich, he get stone ho'se wid plenty servant, he get santegay (counsellor).

"W'en de king hear say he wef get fine son, he rich, well, de king sen' one messenger fo' bring um. Dis messenger he bad man, he wicked; so he tell de king, he say: 'Dis yo' son heah he go take de country f'om yo', ef yo' no kill um.'

"De king say: 'Which punishment yo' go gie um? Gie um special trial, special work fo' do. Ef he no able do um, well, we go kill um.'

"One 'tick (tree) bin deh, he high, en de fruit he sweet, but nobody no dare fo' go up pick um. He get dem antch (ants) wey able fo' sting, dey poison. So de king he messenger say: 'Make de boy mus' pick all dis yeah fruit.'

"De king he 'gree, he sen' call he pickin. W'en he come, de king say: 'Look dah 'tick yandah. Ef yo' kin klim dis 'tick, ef to-morrow mawnin' I meet all dis fruit heah he pick, en deh (there) to one heap bottom de 'tick, I no go kill yo'.'

"De boy say: 'All ret.'

"He go, he tell dis bug-a-bug hill. De bug-a-bug hill tell all dem antch fo' go pick. Dey pick, dey pick tay (till) middle de net. All de fruit dey gadder to one place. Now mawnin' de king meet de fruit all pick. He no talk, he sen' de boy go home.

"Dis bad man he come agin, he tell de king, he say: 'King, yo' bin buy one cow, de cow done multiply, multiply. Ef dey put dem inside place wey dey buil' fo' dem, dey pass one hundred plenty. De boy mus' show de fus' cow wey yo' buy; ef no, he go die.'

"All dis he jus' duh do fo' try kill de boy.

"So de king call he son, he tell um. De boy say: 'All ret, I go come w'en de sun middle de sky; make dem no open de cowfiel'.'

"So de king 'gree. Well, de boy go, he tell de bug-a-bug hill. Well, de bug-a-bug hill see one butterfly, he tell um he mus' do wuk fo' um. So de butterfly tell de boy, he say: 'To-morrow, w'en yo' meet all dem cow form in row, now de cow wey yo' see I fly 'roun' en sit down 'pon, now dis de fus' cow wey de king get.'

"To-morrow de very hour, de boy go. Dem people dey form dem cow, put de fus' cow wey de king buy nah middle dem cow all. W'en de boy 'tan' up, he look de cow fo' moment, he look, he see de butterfly jus' sit down 'pon de cow, he say: 'Ah! Hey! Look de cow middle yandah.'

"All de people wonder fo' see how de boy wise.

"Evenin' tem dis bad man come agin, he no satisfy. He tell de king, he say: 'Make dem dig hole *deep*, make dem put plenty knef, plenty broke bottle all 'roun' de top, all 'roun' de inside; so so knef, so so broke bottle, down, down. Make dem spread mat 'pon top de hole, jus' cover de hole; make dem set chair deh.'

"De king 'gree. Den sen' de same messenger fo' go call de boy. W'en de boy come, dey say dey wan' talk palaver, make he go sit down to dah chair yandah.

"Well, de boy he go near, he 'tan' up, he tell de king, say:

"'I nebber sit down place excep' I take 'tick, chook de place.'

"De king no know how fo' do, he puzzle. He no lek say no, he no lek say yes, so he 'gree. De boy go take long 'tick, de 'tick he heaby. He beat wid um inside de place, de chair fa' down inside hole. De boy no sit down deh, he go home.

"Now de same bad man he come agin to de king, he tell um say: 'Dis now de las' chance wey kin kill yo' son, he no go get out of dis.'

"So de king say: 'All ret.'

"Dey sen' fo' de boy, he distant 'bout some few mile, he come. Dey spread mat 'pon de groun', dey tell um say dey wan' fo' crown um king. Well, de boy bin come wid one of he servant. Dey tell de boy fo' lie down 'pon de mat, dey go wrap um, tie um so he no able fo' loose hese'f; dey lay heaby, heaby stone 'pon um, dey go hebe (throw) um nah wattah, dey go lef um t'ree day. Dey tell um say, now *so* dey kin do fo' crown king.

"Well, dis servant wey bin follow de boy, ef he reach 'tranger place, ef he fo'get anyt'ing, w'en he ready fo' go fo' um, all dem people demse'f kin fo'get somet'ing, dey all kin grap (get up) fo' go fine de t'ing. Well, jus' dey done tie he mastah, en dey ready fo' go hebe um nah dis deep wattah, de servant say: 'Oh, I fo'get somet'ing one mile off.'

"Well, all dem people dey grap, (get up) dey all fo'get somet'ing, dey go. De king se'f he grap, he go. Dey all jus' 'tan' lek crazy.

"Well, w'en dey done go, dis boy heah he call one leelee pickin. De pickin come, he loose all de rope, en de boy come out. He put heaby, heaby stone inside de mat, he tie um tight lek wey de people bin tie um. Well, he go, he go 'way home.

"Now de servant he know say he mastah done go, so he come back, en all dem people come. Dey hase (raise) de mat up, dey t'ink say dat de boy inside, dey go hebe um nah de deep.

"T'ree day dey duh hear drum over to de boy he town, dey hear drum en dance. W'en de t'ree day finis', de boy come to de town, he wear crown, he sit down 'pon hoss, plenty people duh follow um; dey too sit down 'pon hoss, dey rejoice. W'en de boy reach to de town wey he fadder bin, he gadder all dem people; he say he wan' fo' come tell dem de t'ing wey he see w'en he die.

"But dem people no know, dey t'ink say nar (it is) true.

"He tell dem say, w'en he die, aftah dey bin hebe (throw) um nah wattah, he meet de pusson wey crown um king, en dis pusson tell um, say: 'W'en yo' go back, make dey mus' crown de same way dis messenger.' Dat nar de one wey bin try fo' fine all dis trouble fo' de king heen son.

"Dis man yeah, w'en he heah dat, he try fo' run 'way, fo' 'scape, but dey ketch um, dey tie um inside mat, wrap um so he no able fo' loose. Dey lay heaby stone 'pon um, dey go sink um; now he die.

"Dat make he (it is) no good fo' t'ink fo' do bad to yo' cumpin (companion) w'en he innocent."

Dogbah had been restless throughout these stories. They pointed too definite a moral to suit him, and he suspected they had a personal application to some of his own failings.

To change the drift of thought to something more remote, he offered to tell a story he had heard a short time before, while in a distant village.

## An Old Man Turns Elephant.

"Some people deh far up, up Mende country. Dey bin ole too much, dey sick, en all de odder people done tire fo' mine um; dey say dey trouble too much. Now because dis yeah ole pusson no able any mo' fo' do not'ing, dem cumpin (companions) bin kare um nah (into) bush; dey bin brush one place, dey bin buil' one leelee ho'se 'pon top um. But not too good ho'se dey bin buil', dey jus' buil' bamboo roof fo' cover dis yeah ole pusson. Dey bin take four mottah,[58] dey put de ole pusson heen one han' inside one mottah, de odder han' inside odder mottah; one foot dey put inside de mottah wey make t'ree, en de odder foot inside de las' mottah. De mottah-pencil (pestle) dey bin put to heen mout' fo' turn elephan' long, long mout'. Dey take two fannah, dey tie um 'pon he yase (ears). Well, so dey bin lef um; dey go 'way, aftah dey done buil' de ho'se.

"Sometem ef pusson go agin fo' look, dey nebber see um. Well, he done turn elephan'. De foot nar de mottah."

"Nar (is) dat fo' true, true?" asked Konah eagerly, for the transformation appealed strongly to her imagination.

"Dem people say nar true," answered Dogbah, hedging. "Me daddy cousin sister-in-law husban' done see um."

"Man kin turn elephan'," asserted Mammy Yamah decisively. "One tem two girl go nah bush fo' broke wood. Dey hearee monkey wey duh sing one song. One girl hese'f sing de song, he turn elephan'. De odder girl scare, he (she) run go home; he tell dem people all. Dem people beg um sotay (till) he sing de song; he turn elephan'."

An Old Man turns Elephant.

Sobah listened to Mammy Yamah's excited testimony, and then with an air of condescension said: "I tell yo' one story."

## The Man Who Could Not Keep Secrets.

All were ready enough to listen, so the story proceeded:

"One huntin' man bin shoot de elephan' plenty, he bin kill

um, but Elephan' kin turn anyt'ing, he kin turn pusson, beef, (animal) anyt'ing. So one day Elephan' he turn one fine girl, en he come to dis huntin' man yeah. W'en de man see dis fine girl, he drive heen wef, he say: 'Yo' mus' go nah kitchen, go cook.' He no wan' make heen wef hear w'en he en dis girl duh talk.

The Man who could not keep Secrets.

"De girl come ax de man, say: 'How yo' kin manage fo' kill de Elephan'?'

"De man answer, say: 'Look dah gun, he en de bow en arrow

wey bin nah co'ner. I take um; I load um, w'en I see de Elephan' I shoot um, *ding*!'

"Well, de ooman say: 'Ef yo' no get de Elephan'?'

"Den de man say: 'I kin turn to dry 'tick (dead tree), make de Elephan' no see me.'

"Den de girl say: 'But ef de Elephan' mas' (smash) de dry 'tick?'

"Den he tell um say, he kin turn bug-a-bug (ant) hill.

"Den de ooman say: 'Well, ef de Elephan' mas', mas' de bug-a-bug hill? Wey t'ing yo' go do nex'?'

"Well, de wef come nah co'ner, he duh listen w'en dis man tell all him secret. Jus' he wan' tell de girl de las' fing lef', den de wef holler 'pon um, say:

"'Yo'! Yo' tell all de word inside yo'?'

"So he no tell de las' t'ing.

"Den dis ooman go, he turn Elephan' agin.

"De nex' day de man grap (get up), he say he go hunt; he meet dis same ooman done turn Elephan', 'tan' up inside de bush. So he fire. He miss de Elephan', so he turn dry 'tick, lek how he kin do make Elephan' no see um. De Elephan' come mas' de dry 'tick, so he turn bug-a-bug hill. De Elephan' he mas' de bug-a-bug hill. Well, now de las' t'ing lef' wey de man no bin talk. He grap, he go fa' down inside wattah, he turn dat t'ing wey turn fas', fas' 'pon top de wattah. He loss f'om Elephan', but he bin broke, broke all he bone w'en de Elephan' mas' um. F'om dah tem he no come home fo' two day, so heen people go fine um, dey tote (carry) um, bring um nah town. F'om dah tem he no able go huntin' tay (till) he die.

"So ef ooman come to yo', no tell um all de word wey yo' get inside yo' heart; sometem now debble go turn ooman, sometem now Elephan' turn ooman, sometem now snake; yo' no know.

"En no man no fo' do bad to heen wef, because widout heen wef, he bin tell de las' t'ing wey fo' do, make Elephan' no kill um."

"Well," said Sobah, after finishing his story, and noticing that the showers had entirely ceased, "sun duh shine," and with that he arose and walked away with the air of one who knows that he has acquitted himself with credit in the eyes of his fellowmen.

## CHAPTER X

# KONAH TURNS STORY-TELLERT

The next time there was story-telling in Konah's presence, she unwittingly became the chief actor. It came about in this wise. A pack of children, tired of romping, had collected under the projecting roof at the front of Konah's house. Sprawled around in all possible places, and in all conceivable attitudes, they gave their imagination loose reins, and seemed to be trying to outdo one another in the extravagance of their fancies. It was the hour of deep twilight, and the air seemed to palpitate with an invisible life. Mystery and magic seemed but harmonies of the hour.

"Ah, hey!" said Konah excitedly, her eyes dancing and her face glowing with animation, "I get one fine story."

"Pull um!" came in hearty chorus from all around. This is what she told.

## The Devil's Magic Eggs.

"Dis story 'bout two mate (two wives of one husband). De one he die, he lef he pickin to he mate. Dis ooman no lek um, he hate um, he cruel to um. De pickin get wattah, he beat ress (rice), he broke wood, he do eberyt'ing, but w'en he done do all dis, de ooman bin flog um. He yown pickin he no wuk, he no duh do not'ing. So dey do tay (till) de two pickin sick wid yaws. Now de ooman sorry fo' he yown pickin, he no scrub um good; de odder pickin he scrub good, he scrub um wid hatred, but he make de yaws done quick. Now he tire fo' mine dis pickin, he wan' make de debble yeat um.

"One day w'en de pickin go nah de kitchen, he mistake, he t'row 'way (dropped) de ress-'tick nah groun'. So de ooman slap um, he curse, curse um all. De pickin beg, he beg, he say: 'Oh, Mammy, no do me so.'

"De ooman answer: 'No call me mammy, me not to yo' mammy, yo' mammy done die wid witch. I no bin sen' um fo' make he go witch, make he mus' die.' *So* dis wicked ooman duh curse de pickin. Den he tell um, say, he mus' go was' dis 'tick nah de debble heen place, far place. Man mus' take one day fo' reach deh (there) en come back, en leelee pickin no able fo' walker quick lek man. So dis girl he get up, he start, he take de ress-'tick fo' go was' um to dah place wey dah debble bin. W'en de pickin walker 'pon de road, he meet den hoe handle wey bin tie up in bundle; dey get sense fo' talk, dey know one odder. De pickin meet dem handle, dey duh walker, dey ax um: 'Yo'! pickin, which way yo' duh go?'

"He tell um all, say: 'Now me mammy sen' me fo' was' dah ress-'tick.'

"W'en he go agin, he meet one man wey jus' get one grain (single) yi. He ax um, he say: 'Tittie (sissy), which way yo' duh go?'

"De pickin say: 'Me mammy sen' me fo' was' dis ress-'tick.'

"De man show um which way fo' pass. He go tay (till) he reach to de big debble him place. De debble he get so many yi. He get broad head, middle he get bald head. So de debble call um, he say: 'Tittie heah, come feel me louse.'[59]

The Devil's Magic Eggs.

"So de pickin come feel, feel de debble heen louse. De debble get so many yi dat ef de pickin do anyt'ing at all fo' play trick, he kin see, but de pickin no do anyt'ing bad; so de debble take de ress-'tick, he was' um clean, he wrap um wid one silk hankercher, he gie um. Now he tell um say:

"'Go back nah co'ner, take four egg.'

"He duh try dis girl fo' see if he hones'. Plenty big egg bin deh, but de pickin jus' take four; now small, small one he take, he no take de big one. So de debble tell um say:

"'W'en yo' go leelee far yo' mus' bus' one egg, w'en yo' go agin yo' bus' de odder, tay (till) yo' bus' de t'ree, but de las' one yo' bus' um de place wey yo' wan' buil' ho'se.'

"So w'en dis girl go leelee far, he bus' one egg. Now plenty servant en hammock come out fo' kare um go, en plenty box full of clot' en any kind of bead.

"W'en he go agin he bus' de odder one, wey make two; he see officer en sodjer all come out fo' guard um. W'en he go agin he bus' de one wey make t'ree, en behole gold, silver en diamond, en all dem good, good stone, en servant fo' tote (carry) dem. Now de las' egg lef'. W'en he go to one part town wey he wan' fo' buil' ho'se, he bus' de las' egg. Plenty big ho'se come out; fine buildin' en big wall 'roun' dem, en goat, en cow. He go inside, he en he sodjer en he servant all. Dem drum en different, different music all duh play fo' um now."

Of course the interest was intense, while these marvels were being related. Little outbursts of wonder and delight greeted each new revelation, but when, to crown all, there was music of all kinds the children could restrain themselves no longer, but leaped up and performed an impromptu dance.

This, however, was over in an incredibly short time, and the story was allowed to proceed.

"De debble done tell dis girl one t'ing fo' do, fo' make heen mudder come out of de grabe (grave) back. He bin say: 'Bimeby w'en yo' go, yo' mus' pick ress plenty. W'en yo' done beat um yo' soak um, take de mottah en de mottah-pencil to yo' mammy heen grabe, make yo' beat de ress 'pon top de grabe. Wen yo' duh beat so, yo' mus' sing.'

"De pickin do all t'ing lek de debble bin tell um. W'en he duh beat, he duh sing."

At the first mention of "he duh sing", all hands came into position to beat time, and as soon as Konah set the measure, all joined in the rhythmical hand-clapping,

> "Mammy, turn to de wuld back.
> Anyt'ing weh I do, w'en I do um,
> De mammy nebber tankee me.
> He bin jus' flog me, flog me.
> Aftah he flog me done, he say,
> Make I mus' tell um tankee.
> Mammy, come back, come back,
> I duh trouble too much.
> Me mammy come back,
> I done tire of dis mammy."

They easily found a musical note in these lines, however impossible it may appear to any but an African ear. It was a peculiar, quavering, minor strain, full of pathetic pleading.

When the song was ended, the story took its regular course.

"De girl beat, he sing, tay (till) de grabe begin crack, begin open. He sing steady. De grabe 'plit mo', en de mudder head come out. De girl cry, he say: 'Mammy, come back nah wuld.'

"He wan' go grip he mammy, make he draw um come out nah de hole, but de debble bin tell um, say: 'Ef yo' see yo' mammy come out, no draw um; ef yo' draw, he cut middle, en he no come out agin!'

"So de girl no go, he gie de mammy tem, he jus' duh beat, he duh sing

'Mammy, turn to de wuld back.'

"Now de grabe 'plit mo', en de mammy done pull all heen han'. De pickin wan' agin fo' go take heen mammy han', but he no do um, he 'member how de debble bin say: 'Girl, girl, gie yo' mammy tem, he go come nah wuld back agin.' He sing steady:

'Mammy, mammy, sorry fo' me,  
I duh trouble.  
Come back nah wuld,  
Come back.'

"By dis tem de mammy done pull all heen skin, he foot lef'. Now he pull he foot, one foot; de one lef'. De pickin beat, he beat, he beat. Now de mammy all come out. De girl go hole he mudder, take um go inside de ho'se dey get, but befo' he do dis, he bin take dis ress-'tick, he sen' um to he step-mudder, wey bin make um go to de debble place fo' was' de 'tick.

"Well, de step-mudder, w'en he see all de money, en all de fine style, en all de plenty, plenty t'ing wey dis he mate (her associate wife's) pickin get, he do careless, he t'row 'way dis 'tick-'poon 'pon de groun', he tell he yown pickin, he say: 'Make yo' mus' go was' um.'

"But he yown pickin he no train up, he no 'fraid anyt'ing, he no respec' anyt'ing wey he see. So w'en he duh go nah road, he meet de hoe-handle 'tan' up nah road, dey say: 'Tittie (sister), how do?'

"De girl duh vex, he say: 'Make I pass. I nebber see t'ing lek dat, nebber see hoe-handle wey (which) duh talk.'

"Dem 'tick heah bin de debble, wey turn hese'f to different t'ing.

"De pickin go tay (till) he meet de one man wid one yi'. De man say: 'Tittie, how do?'

"De girl vex, he say: 'I nebber see pusson get one yi' middle heen head.' He say: 'Make I pass, I duh go was' me mammy he ress-'tick; no tell me how do.'

"De pickin duh talk bad all to dis man. He go tay he meet de daddy hese'f, se'f, se'f, wey get de wattah side. So de debble call um fo' try um, he say: 'Tittie, come feel me louse.'

"De pickin no know say de debble get plenty yi', so w'en he duh feel dis debble he louse, he see de bald head, he make as ef he wan' fo' conk (strike) um."

Konah gave this little scene with realistic mimicry, and naturally provoked a shout of laughter. As soon as it seemed safe, Konah added: 'He no mean do um, he jus' make trick.'

"De debble he see um, he say: 'All ret', but he no talk. He was' de 'tick-'poon, he no wrap um. W'en he see dis girl nar bad girl, he duh try um agin, he say: 'Now yo' take four egg.'

"So w'en de pickin go to de co'ner, he see dem big, big, big egg, he take um. He get big yi. De debble tell um, say: 'Wen yo' go far leelee bit, yo' mus' bus' de one; w'en yo' go far agin, yo' mus' bus' odder one; w'en yo' go agin, yo' bus' odder; w'en yo' reach to yo' mudder heen ho'se, de las' one yo' bus'.'

"So w'en he go leelee far f'om de debble, he bus' one. Now de honey (bees) come out, dey sting um, dey sting um, dey sting um.

W'en dey tire dey lef um. He go agin, he bus' de one wey make two. Dem snake dey come wrap um all nah (on) he foot, nah he han', nah he neck, nah he wais' all; he no know how fo' do agin. W'en dey done hole um long tem, now dey lef um. W'en he go leelee bit mo', he bus' odder one. So so big man come out, dey get big whip, dey flog um, dey flog um, dey flog um tay dey tire; so dey go. He mammy duh look nah road, he anxious. W'en he pickin come, he see he face all swell. W'en he reach to he mammy heen ho'se, he bus' de las' egg. Now fiah get out, burn de ho'se, burn he mammy en hese'f."

This part of the story was quite as effective as that had been where the other child broke the magic eggs, but the interest, though equally intense, was of a different nature. Never had story heartier reception, or better rendering. Simple young hearts, naturally emotional and responsive, were enchanted by the fairy-tale; and Konah, all a-tremble with excitement, threw all the ardor of her fresh young soul into the telling.

After the exclamations had quieted sufficiently, she added impressively, and with serious gravity:

"Now dis story learn we fo' no do bad to pickin wey no get mammy or daddy."

Other children were anxious to share in the story-telling; and a little girl, seizing the first favorable opportunity, repeated an impossible tale which she had once heard.

## Toothache Entailed.

"Now one boy bin go nah bush fo' cut stick. Well, one ooman bin nah wuld wey get long teet'. Dem people wey (who) duh story, dey say de teet' come out f'om heah, dey reach to Freetown. Well, me wey (who) no duh story, I say dey reach to de end of dis Africa.

"Well, de boy go meet dese teet' heah, he say: 'Dis nar long 'tick.' He begin fo' cut um. De ooman duh holler. De boy hase (raise) he cutlass up, he knock dis 'tick agin—b-o-o-m-katay! De ooman duh holler: 'Me teet' oh, dat nar me teet'!'

Toothache.

"De boy no duh hearee; he cut, he cut. De ooman still duh holler: 'Now me teet', oh! now me teet'!'

"De boy duh cut, he no hearee, he jus' duh cut, en de ooman duh cry. Now he reach close de ooman, en he hearee wey de ooman duh cry: 'Now me teet', oh! now me teet!'

"Now hese'f talk to de ooman, he say: 'Mammy, make I cut um done, he too long.'

"De ooman say: 'But I no go bear, yo' go hurt me too much.'

"De boy say, 'Well, me no duh hearee agin, I duh cut um, I duh finis' um.'

"He cut um tay (till) he reach close de ooman, now; de ooman jus' kin reach de boy, he han' kin grip um. Well, de boy say: 'All ret, I duh lef now. But he no lef, he jus' duh wait leelee bit tay de ooman done forget how he suffer. He go agin, he cut de teet' tay he cut um short inside de mout'. Teet' no bin in de wuld. Nar dat ooman bring teet' nah wuld, en de boy bin cut um, scatter um, he gie all man teet'. Story done."

The story-teller this time was not gifted, and so the story failed to make much of an impression. In the lull that followed, Konah asked: "Yo' know wey t'ing make Spider him middle leelee so?"

They did not know, but were ready to be informed, and Konah was just as ready to tell them. She had heard the explanation from Sobah, only a few days before; so, with the consciousness of having something new to impart, she related this very plausible occurrence.

## Why Mr. Spider's Waist Is Small.

"One tem one king make big dinnah in all him town, en tell all dem beef fo' come yeat. Wen Spider hearee all dis, he greedy too much, he wan' yeat in all dem town yeah, but he no know nah which town dey go cook fus'. So he call all heen pickin, en tell dem 'bout de big dinnah. Dey all glad fo' hearee. Den he take plenty rope, en go wid all heen pickin sotay (till) he reach to de middle of de road; de place wey all dem cross-road meet, wey go to all dem town. He 'tan' up deh. He tie all den rope nah heen middle, en he gie all de end to heen pickin, en tell dem fo' go to all dem town fo' watch. He say de place wey dey cook fus', de pickin mus' draw de rope, so he kin come yeat. But de people done cook nah all dem town de same tem. So w'en dey begin fo' cook, dem pickin begin fo' pull de rope 'tronger de same tem; dey draw all togedder, en so dey draw long tem. Now because all de pickin get 'trenk equal, Spider no go *any* town, he jus' 'tan' up wey de rope meet nah de middle. He no get not'ing fo' yeat dis whole day. De pickin duh draw Spider sotay he middle small, en now dat bin make Spider wais' leelee tay (till) to-day."

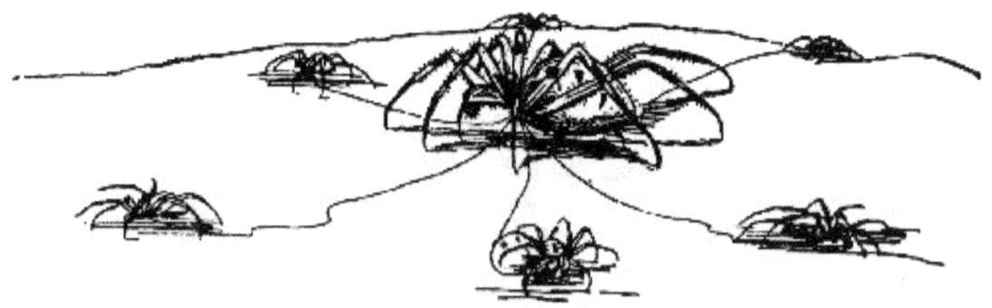

Why Mr. Spider's waist is small.

Just as the story ended, a shrill voice called from another hut, and several "pickins" scudded away to perform the required service. The spell of enchantment was broken by the rude interruption, and could not be conjured back that evening. Not till dreams came, did Konah find herself again in fairy-land.

## CHAPTER XI

# WHILE THE BIRDS DID NOT COME

A few weeks later, near the close of the rainy season, Konah and her mother were at the farm, guarding the ripening rice from the ravages of birds and other marauders. Two look-out towers, each about six feet high, stood on commanding elevations near each end of the field. From the tops of these towers the women kept watch, frightening away the birds with stones, and slings, and metal rattles. It was now early afternoon, and the birds were taking a rest until time for their evening repast. Konah's longing for companionship led her to abandon her tower, and go over to the one occupied by her mother, who must have sympathized with the child's feelings, for she did not scold, or drive her back to the neglected duty, but allowed her to settle down and indulge her propensity for dreaming.

Konah's natural love for the magical, marvellous and romantic, had been intensified by the experiences of the preceding weeks and months, until it had become a controlling passion, so, thinking this a favorable opportunity, she teased her mother for stories, until that good-natured soul was forced to comply.

The first story was all the more pleasing to the girl because it related to her prime favorites, Mr. Spider and Cunning Rabbit. In her own peculiar crooning tone, Mammy Mamenah told her tale.

## Mr. Spider Secures A Powerful Witch Medicine.

"Well, Spider bin to heen facki (village), he en Cunnie Rabbit. One day dey go to Freetown. Spider buy gun en powder. Well, dah tem all dem beef dey no know 'bout gun en powder. Dey all bin lib nah town lek pusson; dey lib inside ho'se, all beef (animals) get heen (their) yown. Den ho'se wey dey get, den plenty. Well, w'en Spider come nah evenin' tem, he holler loud, he say he get witch med'cin' fo kill dem people wey get witch. He say: 'Nobody fo' come out all dis net, because de med'cin' go walk all 'bout dis town', he say: 'I no bizzen, oh, ef he go kill anybody.'[60]

"All dem people den 'gree, den say: 'Oh, Daddy, make dat t'ing wey yo' talk true, make de witch people finis' nah dis town, because dey plenty, oh!'

"So Spider, w'en net come, he load he gun, he ram um. W'en all de town silence he come out, he bootoo (crouched) nah Deer he do'-mout', because Deer he stupid pass (beyond) all beef. Spider done ready wid he gun. Well, Deer open de do' fo' come outside, Spider shoot he gun, 'b-o-o-m!' De noise he loud; Deer fa' down, he done die. Spider he run, he go inside ho'se, he lock de do', he holler, he say:

"'Hay-ee, hay-ee! Oonah (you) see wey I bin tell yo' 'bout de witch wey bin inside dis town? Mr. Deer hese'f get witch.'

"W'en de beef all hearee de big, big noise, dey t'ink say dis med'cin' wey Spider bring duh fet wid witch. Den say: 'How Spider bin know? He deh inside ho'se, he do' lock; dah med'cin' get power fo' true, make he kare 'way dem witch all.'

Mr. Spider secures a powerful Witch Medicine.

"Spider go tote (carry) him big, big beef, wey he kill, he kare um go nah ho'se, he cook um. De pot—de pusson wey bin lie, he say he big lek dis town Rotifunk, but me wey nebber lie, I put leelee salt make he sweet, I say he big lek Freetown, Temne country, Mende country. Spider he cook all de beef. He, he wef en he pickin yeat um all de same net. De nex' net Spider come out agin, he go to Mr. Elephan', he go watch to de do' wid he gun; he put two-tem as much inside he gun as wey he bin put yesterday. Aintee yo' know Elephan' big?

"So w'en Elephan' jus' peep, he wan' fo' come out, now Mr. Spider he lay um, he shoot, gbe-gbe-e-n!! Elephan' fa' down, he done die. Spider he run go inside ho'se, he holler agin, he say de same word lek how he bin say 'bout Mr. Deer. He take de beef, he go cook um. Fo' two day, to-morrow en nex' to-morrow, nobody no hear any witch, oh! because Elephan' he big. Now dis bin hangry tem, so make Spider pull dis cunnie 'bout witch. He go nex' tem to Mr. Lepped, he say:

"'Dah fat fellay!'(Because he kin yeat plenty animal, he rich, he skin full plenty palm-ile.[61]) 'Dah fellay deh, I go kare um to-morrow.'

"He go sit down close Lepped he do'-mout', he cock he gun, he ready. W'en Lepped go come out nah net, Spider lay um, he shoot um de same, he run go nah ho'se, he talk de same word lek befo'. So Spider do sot-a-y (till) dem beef dey lef few, no mo'. Well, so he bin kill dem beef ebery net, ebery net. One mawnin' he go to de fa'm. Mr. Cunnie Rabbit come now, he see dat Spider he absen', so he go inside he ho'se, he say: 'Make I go see de med'cin' wey Spider get fo' kill all we people;' he *say*, 'Nar witch pusson he duh kill.' He peep, he see gun, he look one side, he see bag hang wid powder inside, en all t'ing, he kare um go home to he yown ho'se.

"W'en Spider come home, he look, he no see anyt'ing, he say: 'Ah, m-o-nay! Mese'f done los'.'

"Evenin' tem Spider lay down, but he no able fo' sleep. He grap (get up), he go open de do', he run out. Well, Cunnie Rabbit done ready fo' shoot, but too much eagerness, he miss Spider; de gun shoot odder way. Spider holler, he say: 'What pusson shoot deh so?' Cunnie Rabbit answer, he say:

"'Yo' say yo' duh drive 'way witch, en behole yo' bin shoot all we people.'

"Spider say: 'Ah, shut mout' one tem! Make we be one word, we two be cumpin (companions).' So de Cunnie Rabbit he 'gree.

"W'en dem beef dey see de witch med'cin' wan' fo' kill dem

all, dey all scatter, go nah bush. So Spider make dem beef no duh lib nah town, dey all duh scatter nah bush tay to-day."

This story only whetted Konah's appetite, and so she insisted on hearing another one at once.

"Ah, yo' humbug too much," protested Mamenah, but at the same time she began to search her memory for another story. Finally she said: "Well, I tell yo' 'bout Spider en de ole ooman."

## Mr. Spider Gets Into Trouble Again.

"One ole ooman get one sheep. Because dis ooman ole, he no able fo' walker, so he say he go gie de sheep to any pusson wey go tote (carry) um. So de news go all 'roun de country. People come, dey look de ooman good fashion, but de heart no gie dem fo' take de wuk. So w'en Spider hear dat, he go to de place, he ax de ooman fo' de wuk. De ooman he tell um all t'ing, en Spider he 'gree fo' take de job. He take de sheep f'om de ooman, he kill um, he yeat um, he say he go tote (carry) de ooman any way wey de ooman wan' fo' go. But Spider he no know say dat sometem de ooman he han' long, sometem he short, same way wid he foot. He able fo' make dem any way wey he lek. W'en he han' long good fashion, he 'tan' lek one ole palm-tree fo' long; same way wid he foot. So w'en Spider done kill dis sheep, w'en he done yeat um, de ooman tell um say:

"'I wan' fo' go nah one odder town, make yo' come tote me.'

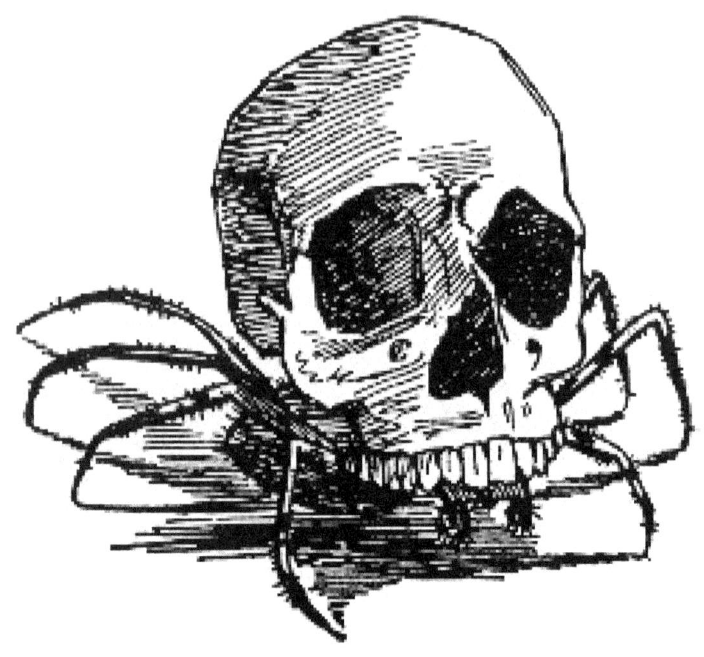

Mr. Spider gets into Trouble again.

"W'en Spider hase (raise) de ooman, put um 'pon he back, de ooman make all he han' en he foot long, he wrap Spider two, t'ree tem, four tem. Spider no know how fo' do agin, en he no able fo' run 'way; de ooman done hole um so he no able fo' lef um. But Spider he cunnie, he nebber lef nah (in) trouble. W'en dey done go far nah road, he ax de ooman, he say:

"'Wey t'ing yo' 'fraid pass (beyond) all t'ing dis wuld?'

"De ooman say: 'De t'ing I 'fraid pass all, bin dem Manekky,[62] dem cut-nose people.'

"So w'en dey go nah road, w'en he tote de ooman, he hearee den woodcock wey duh talk: 'Wah, wah, wah!', so he say:

"'Look, Mammy, dem Manekky people duh come.'

"De ooman 'fraid *bad*, he say: 'Kare me go, hide me! Make dem pass befo' we go.'

"So Spider he lef' de road, he tote de ooman inside de bush, he kare um bottom one big 'tick (foot of a tree). Now de ooman come down f'om he back. Spider tell de ooman, say:

"'Make I go look ef dey done pass.'

"So w'en Spider go, he no go to de ooman agin, he jus' laugh de ooman, he go. He no come agin bottom de 'tick fo' look de ooman.

"W'en 'bout eight moon done pass, Spider en he fren' wey he wan' make he wef, dey duh walker nah de same road. Spider wan' fo' do trick fo' make dis girl laugh, he say:

"'Wait me nah road, I go come.'

"So he go to dis place wey he lef' dis ooman; de ooman done die long tem. W'en he wan' bootoo (stoop over) fo' make he take de ooman he dry head (skull), fo' make he go scare he fren', de dry head jus' joomp one tem, he fashin 'pon he nose. Well, he try fo' pull dis dry head 'pon top he nose, but he no able. De girl wey lef' nah road, he call um t-a-y, but Spider shame fo' come wey de girl kin look um. W'en he try, try agin long tem fo' pull de dry head, he no able, so he come out nah de road wid de dry head 'pon top he nose. W'en de ooman see um, he 'fraid bad. F'om dat tem he say he no wan' Spider agin.

"Spider try fo' pull dis t'ing 'pon top he nose, he no wan' kare um go nah town; he shame, bimeby people go see um, but de dry head too 'trong, Spider mus' kare um go nah town. He go to de blacksmit', en de blacksmit' go take hot iron, he pull de dry head 'pon top he nose.

"So ef yo' wan' take any wuk f'om pusson, yo' mus' look de pusson *good*, en make yo' know de wuk wey yo' wan' do, ef yo' able fo' do um. Bimeby ef yo' begin do de wuk, yo' lefum, yo' wan' do rascal trick, yo' get trouble lek Spider."

As Mamenah finished the story, a flock of over zealous birds swooped down upon the rice-field, intent upon securing an early evening meal, but the woman, keeping a vigilant eye in that direction, started up with the cry:

"Eh! lookee, see dem bird. Come make we dribe um."

Much shouting, shaking of rattles and hurling of stones soon frightened away the birds. Mamenah grumbled on for some time about the troublesome pillagers, but Konah fell to dreaming about Mr. Spider and the difficulty resulting from the cruel trick he played on the old woman. There was something uncanny and suggestive of spirits in the way the skull had behaved. Suddenly, and as if the light of a new truth had dawned upon her, the child asked:

"Mammy, yo' t'ink say nar true word dey bin talk w'en dey say die pusson kin walker nah wuld?"

Mamenah looked thoughtfully into the little girl's face before making any reply. Finally she said:

"Die man kin walker, kin dance, kin do all t'ing lek pusson. Some tem he kin come, kin go, kin make noise, but no man no able fo' see um."

Konah was deeply interested in a being that could make itself visible or invisible at pleasure, and accordingly pushed her questions further.

Mamenah, like a wise teacher, chose to answer all by relating a story in point.

## A Ghost Story.

"One tem one country bin deh. Dem people wey get dis country, dey lek fo' dance Wongko (Purro devil dance). Well, odder people f'om odder country kin come dance wid um. Well, dem people wey come out f'om de odder country fo' dance, dey all get fren' (sweethearts), so w'en dey wan' fo' go back to den place, den fren' kin follow um leelee way, go lef den nah road. So dey bin do all de tem. But one ooman bin deh, he lek he fren' too much.

"One day w'en den 'tranger come dance nah de town, w'en dey go back, all man (every one) go lef he fren' nah road. W'en dey duh go, one dog go wid dem nah road. Dey done go leelee far, den some of dem young man, dem tell den fren' 'Goodbye', dem say:

"'We go meet nex' moon.'

"Some of dem ooman go back, but some tell den fren', say:

"'Any way wey yo' go nah wuld, we all go *go*; ef now yo' die, we all go die.'

"Well, w'en dey go far agin, dey reach to one big, big valley. Now all den man dey tell den fren' wey bin say dey go die wid um, dey say:

"'Oonah go back. W'en de nex' moon kin white, we go come agin.'

"So dey all go back. But one no go, he say he mus' follow sotay he reach dah place wey he fren' bin lib. De dog deh wid de ooman. Dah man tell de ooman, he say: 'Go back!'

"De ooman say: 'No!'

"De man say: 'I lek yo' too much, lef nah town. W'en I come

back I go come to yo', but no follow me to dah place wey we duh go.'

"Dah ooman say: 'I go *go*!'

"Well, dis ooman no know say dis man nar (is) die pusson, oh! W'en dey kin get dance nah town, den die pusson all, dey kin come out den grabe (grave), dey come dance wid dem people, but dem people nebber know quick fo' say dey bin die pusson. But w'en dey know, dey tell all de ooman, dey say:

"'W'en pusson come out far country, come dance, oonah no mus' go wid um; sometem bimeby dey die pusson, yo' no know.'

"Dis girl too, dey bin tell um, say: 'Die pusson kin come out de grabe fo' dance, so no get fren' wey come out far 'way.'

"But de ooman he get 'tronger yase,[63] en he get dis heah die pusson fo' fren'.

"W'en dey done go sotay (far) den odder die pusson done los', den gone to de grabe, but de one man lef'. He en dis girl den go to heen town, but de ooman no know say dis die man town. W'en dey go, dey reach nah net, but den jus' meet one ho'se nah de place. Well, de girl see de place white, no mo', because soso (merely) die pusson wey get white clo'es bin deh. Well, de man done los' f'om he han', en dis ooman he dey inside de one ho'se. Den die pusson jus' come curse um, suck teet' 'pon um, no mo', but de ooman done 'fraid, he no get nobody. He see white clo'es, no mo'; den come suck teet', den los' agin; he hearee um, he no see pusson. But oonah no know dog get witch yi? He duh see den die people heah, he begin fo' holler 'pon dem fo' make dem go back. Well, dis dog yeah he turn pusson, he ax de ooman, he say:

"'Ef I pull yo' f'om dis trouble yeah, ef yo' go home, yo' cook fo' yo' fren', en I go tief all de ress en de fis'—ef yo' call me *dog* yo' go die.'

"He no wan' de girl call um dog, because he done turn pusson.

"De girl 'gree, he say: 'Come go, kare me back.'

"De dog done turn dog agin, so he able fo' holler 'pon dem die pusson. He 'tan' up befo', w'en dem die pusson come, he holler 'pon dem, en dem go back. Well, w'en dis girl en dis dog go far nah road, dey no know de country, den meet one big, big wattah, den no know how fo' cross um, en de dog say: 'Come, lay down 'pon me back.'

"So de girl lay down, en de dog cross um over dah big, big wattah. W'en dey done cross de ooman tell de dog 'Tankee, tankee.' Long tem he tankee um.

"Well, den de dog say: 'I 'gree fo' de tankee, but yo' no mus' call me name dog, oh! w'en yo' go to de town, oh! but yo' fo' gie me odder fine name lek pusson.'

"He no wan' turn pusson w'en he reach de town, because de people go ax de girl: 'Which side de dog done go, wey bin follow yo'?'

"Well, dah dog kare de ooman sotay (till) dey done reach nah home. De ooman tell he people all dah trouble wey he see, he say:

"'Dah t'ing wey follow we two, so, he sabe (save) me;' but he no call he name dog. Well, dis girl people kin do dis dog good. No matter fo' de people ef dey call um dog, but only de girl no mus' call um dog. Well one day dah ooman cook fine sweet ress fo' he fren', not fo' de die pusson, but odder fren' in de town. W'en he done cook um, w'en he go call he fren' fo' come yeat dah ress, w'en he come back he meet dah t'ing done yeat um. He no talk anyt'ing, he go cook odder ress, he gie he fren'. Well, dah dog duh yeat de ress wey de girl cook, all de tem. One day he done vex 'pon de dog. He cook one fine ress wid fat beef fo' he good fren' nah de town. Well, w'en he go call he fren', he meet dah dog done yeat dah sweet, sweet ress, en he lay down close de bowl wey he done yeat. Dah ooman vex, he say:

"'Dah dog tief me ress all de tem, look how he come tief me ress wey I cook fo' me fren'.'

"Wen de girl call um dog, de dog look um, en de girl fa' down, he die. Story done."

After a brief silence, Mamenah said: "Make yo' go back, now, dem bird go come agin."

Without a further word, the two watchers turned again to their duties, the woman thinking of rice-pots and fish, and the child of white shadowy forms that come and go through an invisible village.

## CHAPTER XII

# A HARVEST HOME IN TEMNE-LAND

The rice is now ripe for the harvest. Sobah has engaged the services of a half dozen sturdy men to aid in gathering the crop. Neighbors and friends, many of them women, have assembled to take part in celebrating the occasion, for rice harvest is a time of much ceremony and rejoicing.

The work is about to begin. The men are lined up at the end of the field, each with a sharp knife in his hand. Behind them stand two large boys with drums, and along the side of the field are gathered the neighbors, ready to do their part. The drums begin to beat, and the knives of the men to fly rapidly, cutting off the heads of the rice, while a peculiar swinging of the body keeps time to the music. Across the field the procession moves, the drums following close after the harvesters, and keeping up a continual beating, often rapid and work-inspiring. The men are dressed in special harvest garb for the occasion. On their heads are bright colored caps trimmed up in gorgeous style, while one is of coarse black hair in tiniest braids deftly joined. Around the loins a small piece of cloth is wound. Fastened to arms, legs, and bodies are strings, from which dangle ornaments that quiver in the air, as the bodies sway in time to the music. The men continually keep up a harvest song, while the women join in, clapping their hands in unison with the movement.

Thus the harvest is gathered to the sound of music and the song of rejoicing.

About five o'clock the work of the day is ended. The men retire to the farm-house to a bountiful feast of boiled rice and fowl-stew prepared by Mamenah, with the aid of other women. After their appetites were fully satisfied, the men gathered in a group at the foot of a great tree, to await the rising of the moon before returning to the village. All were in the best of spirits, and there was much good-natured chaffing and jesting. Sobah, who was well pleased with the day's results, knowing the fondness of the men for the stories he could tell so delightfully, said finally:

"Yo' do well, to-day; I go tell yo' story, now."

It was a generous offer, and the men were not slow in accepting it.

## Watch-Pot And Greedy.

It was his desire to please the men, that led Sobah to choose this particular story. They could appreciate to the full every new move in the contest of wits, and expressed this appreciation by peals of laughter and boisterous exclamations. Sobah himself preserved a show of decorum, only giving way now and then to a pleased chuckle over some particularly clever trick. The story, minus the tone, facial expression and gestures was as follows:

"Well, one man bin east, one bin wes'. De one wey bin east he greedy, de one wey bin wes' he duh Watch-pot.[64] Now de greedy one he hear 'bout de one wey duh Watch-pot, en he say: 'No matter how dis man kin Watch-pot, he no go yeat me yown yeat.' Now Watch-pot he hear 'bout how dis man greedy, no 'tranger ever yeat to um, nobody ever yeat heen yeat. Now he say: 'I mus' yeat he ress.' So one day he say he go go to de east to de greedy man. Well, w'en he wan' go he buy clo'es,[65] all kind of clo'es; he get box, he put de clo'es in de box. He take all t'ing wey de carpenter need, en sawyer all; nail, tool, en all t'ing. Den he get up, he start off, he go. He go far to de east wey de greedy man bin nah heen fa'm-ho'se. De day w'en he go reach, de greedy man done hear say he come, he no far 'way 'pon de road. De same day now, dis greedy man heah, he kill big bush-hog, he' jus' shabe (divide) de meat middle part, he wef cook plenty, nearly all, he cook half wid de ress. Well, jus' he cook so, dey see dis Watch-pot man he tell 'How do', he say, 'Brudder, how do?'

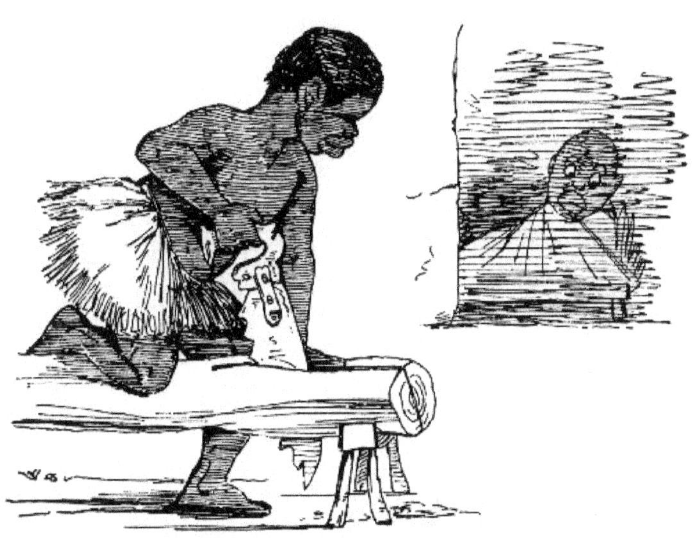

Watch-Pot and Greedy.

"Dis heah man he say: 'How do, sit down, now.'

"So de 'tranger sit down, he open he box, he pull one piece clo'es, he tell dis man heah, 'How do', wid de clo'es. He ax, he say: 'Wey yo' name?'

"He answer um, say: 'Me name Greedy; wey yo' yown name?'

"Dat one answer: 'Me name Watch-pot, I come tell yo' How do.' Because I bin heah 'bout yo', I come tell yo' How do.'

"De greedy man say: 'All ret, go nah town now, I go meet yo' deh bimeby.'

"De Watch-pot say: 'How I go do? I no know anybody nah de town 'cept yo'. Make I wait evenin' tem, make we two go togedder.'

"Dey sit down *all day*. De ress sit down close de fire side.

"De man he call he wef, he tell um, he say: 'Dis man heah no go yeat dis ress.'

"Den leelee pickin dey duh cry, hangry ketch dem. Dey all sit down dey tay (till) young evenin' tem. Well, de man he call he wef nah (from) de room; dem pickin dey cry, he no know how fo' do agin. So he tell he wef, he say: 'I go lay down, I say I sick. W'en he stay leelee bit, I do lek I die. Den make yo' go tell de people in de town say I done die. Bimeby so, jus' de man go', I go grap, (get up) we go yeat de ress.'

"Well, de man he lay down, he say he sick. Leelee bit, no mo', now de daddy he die, but not to *true* die.

"Well, now de ooman he go tell de man, he say:

"'Daddy, how we go do now? Yo' jus' come tell yo' brudder how do to-day, en look; he done die. Go now, tell de people wey in de town say he done die.'

"De man say: 'Ee, ee! Yo' wey bin ooman, aintee yo' nar ooman, aintee yo' fo' come out wid holler?[66] Go nah de town, tell dem people all. Me, wey man, make me lef close me brudder; lef me fo' mine um tay yo' come.'

"Den de ooman say: 'Well, who go was' um?'

"De man say: 'I go was' um, he now me brudder, I no 'fraid um.'

"Den de man go was' um all. De ooman say: 'Go nah town, make yo' buy white clo'es.'

"De man say: 'Wait me.' He open he box, he pull de white clo'es.

"De ooman he say: "W'en me man die, he say make me make[67] coffin fo' um. Make yo' go buy boa'd.'

"De man say: 'Make yo' get up f'om dah 'tick wey yo' sit down 'pon.' He put one bench heah, he put one yandah, he take de 'tick, he put um 'pon top, he open he box, he take he saw, he saw all de 'tick, he make boa'd. Den he nail de coffin all.

"De ooman duh watch, he duh t'ink: 'Wey t'ing I go do now fo' sabe (save) me man?' He say: 'Me man say, w'en he die, make dem make windah to he head, fo' pull he neck, come out.'

"De man make all.

"De ooman say: 'Well, make we wait nah mawnin' now, befo' we bury de man.'

"Dis tem dark done come, en still de ress 'tan' up close de fire side. De ooman say: 'Well, how we go do fo' wood fo' make fiah?'

"De man say: 'Dem piece, piece boa'd, heah.'

"He come out do'-mout', he pick, pick all dem 'tick, he make big fiah all net, make big fiah tay do' clean. W'en do' clean, de wef say:

"'Make yo' dig hole, make we go bury me man nah bush *yandah*.'

"He jus' wan' make de 'tranger go, fo' make dem lef yeat de ress.

"Den de man say: 'Ee! Me brudder wey get dis fa'm, yo' wan' go bury um inside de bush deh?' He say: 'Now inside dis fa'm-ho'se I go bury um.[68] W'en I done, I go fix de flo' so pusson no know se'f, eh!'

"Well, de ooman say: 'Make yo' come out en go behine de ho'se, I wan' fo' tell me man goodbye.'

"W'en he done go, de wef tell de man, he say: 'Dis yeah 'tranger go bury yo' heah fo' yo' yown yeat. Make yo' get up, make we yeat de ress.'

"De man say: 'Lef fo' talk; me ress he no go yeat um. Make yo' hide de hoe, make he go nah town fo' fine hoe fo' come dig me grabe.'

"De ooman say: 'All ret.'

"Now de man come inside back. De ooman go hide de hoe, but de man no see w'en he hide um. De ooman say: 'We no get hoe, how we go manage? Make yo' go nah town fo' get hoe, fo' come dig de grabe.'

"De man he say: 'Wait me.' He open he box, he pull dem digger wid shovel; he *dig*, he *dig*, he *dig*; de hole he deep. He go inside hole, de hole cover um all. De man he cunnie lek rabbit. He go inside, he come out quick. W'en he come out he put de coffin, he say: 'Make yo' tell um goodbye; ef yo' done, I go put um inside de coffin.'

"De ooman say: 'Go back behine de ho'se, I wan' fo' talk to um.'

"Well, de man he come out, but he no go far 'way, jus' 'roun' de ho'se. De ooman say: 'Get up, dis man go bury yo', get up!'

"De ress duh 'tan' up, de pickin duh cry, but not fo' den daddy; dey duh cry fo' de ress, because de hangry duh ketch dem. W'en de ooman tell he man make he get up, ef not, de 'tranger go bury um, he say: 'Lef me, make he bury me, but he no yeat me ress.'

"De Watch-pot man come inside, he take de Greedy man, he put um inside coffin, but he neck lef', because window bin lef' wey de head come out. W'en he put de coffin inside de hole 'traight-way, de ooman say: 'No put um 'traight, make he 'tan' up.'

"Now de man take de coffin, he turn um over fo' make de head down. De ooman say: 'No, put um make de head up.'

"So de man put de head up. W'en he done put de coffin, he begin fo' cover um wid de dirty (earth); he cover all 'roun', de neck lef', no mo'; he cover all 'roun' to de coffin. Now de ooman tell de man, he say: 'Come out, make me tell me man goodbye fo' de las' tem now.'

"Watch-pot come out, de ooman tell he man, say: 'Come out, dis man go bury yo', eh!'

"He answer he wef, say: 'Lef me, make he bury me, he no go yeat me ress.'

"Well, now de man come fo' cover de half part wey lef', no mo'; he know say ef he jus' cover um, de man go come out de grave w'en he done go. De las' shovel lef' now. Well he dip de dirty hard fo' make he cut de man inside de hole, fo' make he kill um. De die man open he yi leelee w'en he see wey t'ing he cumpin wan' fo' do. He say yo' betty pull me; but me ress, yo' no go yeat um, ef nar fo' dat yo' do dis t'ing.'

"So de man pull um. De greedy man heen wef say: 'Take up de ress, make we yeat um all. Den he tell de Watch-pot man, say: 'Go gie me dat calabas' wey 'tan' up yandah.'

"De place far leelee bit, en befo' de man come back wid de calabas' so, Greedy tell he wef fo' take de ress, hese'f take de soup, en dey run inside de bush. Behole w'en dey run, dey fo'get de calabas' en de 'tick-'poon fo' dish up de ress. Den Watch-pot take de 'tick-'poon en de calabas', he run aftah dem; he go, he meet dem, he see dey go behine one big 'tick. Jus' dey done sit down deh, now de ooman say: 'Look, we no get calabas' en 'poon fo' take up, eh!'

"Jus' now de Watch-pot come, he say: 'Aintee dis de 'tick en de calabas' wey yo' fo'get? I done bring um.'

"De ooman say: 'Fetch um.' De man say: 'Make yo' come yeat.' He no know how fo' do agin, but he vex when he talk so.

"De Watch-pot man come, dey yeat all de ress. W'en dey finis' fo' yeat, de Watch-pot man say: 'Tankee, tankee de pusson wey cook de ress.'

"De man done vex, he say: 'Me no cook um.'

"Den de man say: 'Well, tankee de pusson wey soak de ress.'

"De Greedy man say: 'Me no soak um.'

"De Watch-pot man say: 'Well, tankee de man wey brush de fa'm, plant um.'

"De Greedy man answer um: 'Yo' no get bizzen deh, I no plant um.'

"Watch-pot say: 'Well, how yo' bin do?'

"He answer um: 'I no know, no ax me not'ing.'

"Den de Watch-pot man say: 'Well, goodbye.'

"Greedy answer um, say: 'Ef yo' lek, yo' no go; ef yo' lek yo' go', I no get bizzen deh.'

"So Watch-pot take all he t'ing, he go *pong*!

"Now dem two pusson deh, which one pass fo' cunnie?"

The delight of the men over the narrative of Watch-pot and Greedy was so genuine and keen, that Sobah quite readily consented to tell another story. While trying to think of something appropriate, his eye fell upon an axe that was leaning against a post of the farm-house. The axe itself was a novelty in that part of the country, a result of one of Sobah's trips to the coast.

"Yo' see dah axe yandah?" he asked, pointing to the article in question. "Yo' no know which side he come out? Well, I tell yo' 'bout um."

The Origin of the Axe.

## The Origin Of The Axe.

"Now one boy en one girl bin deh. De boy kin stone plenty bird, he kill one. De girl go take de bird wey de boy get, he yeat um. Den de boy cry fo' de bird, en de girl take one corn, he giē um. De boy go put de corn nah groun, en de bug-a-bug (ants) yeat um. Den he cry 'pon de bug-a-bug, de bug-a-bug make one country-pot, gie um. He take de country-pot, he go get wattah, en de wattah take de country-pot 'way f'om he han'. So he cry 'pon de wattah, en de wattah gie um fis'. He go put de fis' 'pon de sho', en de 'awk kare um go. He call de 'awk name, en de 'awk take one he wing, he gie um. W'en he put de wing 'pon 'tick, de breeze come take um, en he cry 'pon de breeze, he sing:

"'Dah breeze take me wing, eh!'"

With the first line of the song, the story-teller's voice fell into a chanting movement, and he began beating time with hand and foot. The movement was contagious, and soon every hand was clapping noisily.

> "'Dah breeze take me wing, eh!
> De wing wey de 'awk done gie me;
> 'Awk done yeat me fis', eh!
> Dah fis' wey wattah gie me;
> Wattah take me pot, eh!
> Dah pot wey de bug-a-bug gie me;
> Bug-a-bug yeat me corn, eh!
> De corn wey dah girl bin gie me;
> Girl yeat me bird, eh!
> Wey *mese'f* bin ketch um.'

"Now de breeze go pick plenty fruit fo' de boy, en de babboo (baboon) take de fruit, yeat um. He cry 'pon de babboo, en de babboo take axe, he gie um. De boy kare de axe go nah town; de chief take um f'om he han'. W'en de chief take um f'om he han', he cry 'pon de chief, he say:

"'Me poor boy, I suffer! I ketch one bird, girl yeat um. W'en I tell um, he gie me one corn. I take um, put um down en bug-a-bug yeat um. I cry 'pon dah bug-a-bug, bug-a-bug gie me one country-pot. I go get wattah wid um, wattah take um f'om me han'. I cry 'pon de wattah, wattah gie me one fis'. I take de fis', I put um 'pon de sho', 'awk take um 'way. I cry 'pon de 'awk, 'awk gie me one wing. I take de wing, I put um down, breeze take um. I cry 'pon de breeze, breeze pick plenty fruit fo' me. Babboo take um f'om me han'. I cry 'pon babboo, babboo gie me axe. W'en I fetch um nah town, *yo'* wey bin gentry, yo' take um f'om me han'. Well, wey t'ing I go do now?'

"Well, de chief answer um back, he say:

"'Dis kind of t'ing no bin to dis town, so I go take um. I gie yo' lot of me money, fo' make I go take dis axe.'

"He answer de chief back, he say:

"'Well, befo' yo' take um, not to leelee bit money yo' gie me, yo' gie me *plenty*, because I bin suffer fo' de axe; I cry 'pon all dem t'ing befo' dey gie me de axe.'

"Well, de chief answer um back, he say: 'I gie yo' money en make yo' sit down to dis town so yo' no suffer. I gie yo' plenty slave.'

"He answer de chief, he say: 'All ret.'

"De chief take plenty money, he gie um wid slave. Well, de boy take de axe, he gie um to de chief, en de chief tankee um. De chief take de axe, he make de blacksmit' look de axe. Dey follow how de ax bin make, en dey make one, but he no so good lek de fus' one. Befo' dis tem heah, axe no bin to dis wuld.

"De chief say: 'Make de boy mus' go cry agin, make de babboo show um how fo' do wid de axe, ef he fo' make hole in um, hang um nah he neck.'

"Den de boy say: 'Chief, ef yo' no wan' de axe, gie me back, make I no go die agin. Ef I go back I go die, because dah place *bad* wey I bin suffer.'

"De chief take de axe, he say: 'All ret.' He say: 'Make yo' no go agin.' He get one Kongah man (magician) to he town. De Kongah man show um how fo' do wid de axe fo' 'plit wood. Well, w'en he done show um so, he say: 'All ret.'

"So all man make axe tay dey sabbee (know) fo' make um. Now dey scatter um all over dis wuld."

The men found but little occasion in this story for their usual outbursts of laughter, but they were none the less charmed with the strange chain of events by which the axe was brought into existence. "Story done," Sobah remarked, as the narrative ended, and with that he arose, and picking up his much prized axe, set out for the village.

CHAPTER XIII

# KONAH HAS A WONDERFUL DAY

One forenoon, two weeks after the rice harvest, the little village was thrown into a state of intense excitement by the news which a messenger had just brought. "White ooman duh come," was the word that passed from mouth to mouth. Scarcely a half dozen of the inhabitants of the village had seen a white woman, and not more than a third of them had seen a white man, therefore with the approach of two white women and three white men, and their carriers and attendants, curiosity and fear wrought the people up to the highest pitch of expectancy. A miscellaneous company of men, women and children, Konah foremost among them, gathered at the edge of the village to stare at the strangers as they entered. The procession that was approaching was rather imposing. The five white people in hammocks, each hammock supported on the heads of four carriers, and a score of other attendants made up the train. Just as they came opposite the group of natives, one of the missionaries, with the kindest of intentions, looked benevolently around at the people, with results quite contrary to his expectations. One old man uttered a cry of terror, ran into a hut and hid himself, and could not be coaxed out while the strangers were in town. Even Konah shrank back, and felt inclined to run. The interpreter soon discovered that the glasses worn by the missionary had occasioned all this alarm. Superstitious imagination transformed these simple pieces of glass into a dangerous witch medicine, that would enable the wearer to blast with dreadful curses the lives of all upon whom he might look, so the harmless glasses had to be laid aside.

The procession moved on to the barreh, where the white people were left while a messenger went to inform the chief. That personage soon appeared in his native dignity, and on being introduced, touched fingertips with each of the white people, who said "How do" to him with pieces of cloth. He welcomed them with the big-hearted hospitality characteristic of his tribe, and called them his "strangers" (guests). Huts were vacated in order to furnish lodgings; and short, quick orders, called out to right and left, sent the people scurrying away to procure rice and fowls for the use of the visitors. Meanwhile a crowd of natives was banked around the barreh, looking on with undisguised wonder. Konah was mounted on the mud wall, taking in every detail with all absorbing interest. A missionary told the chief that if he would call a meeting of his people, they would talk to them the "God-word." The summons was given, and now Konah had another ravishing experience. The carriers had brought out a little organ which the party carried for the purpose of attracting the people. One of the white women sat down before it, ran her fingers over the keys, and lo, the strangest music Konah's ears had ever heard. Then the white people and their followers sang a tender hymn. Konah was so entranced that she forgot herself and her surroundings. She came behind the organist, moved her hands in the air in imitation of the player's movements, and opened her mouth in an unconscious effort to join in the singing. At the close of the services, the interpreter announced that in the evening the white man would again talk the "God-word", and would show "plenty picture." The curious crowd then followed to the barreh, and watched the preparations for dinner. The meal itself brought the greatest revelations yet witnessed. Wonder of wonders, the white men and women ate at the same time, nay, even the men seemed to serve the women, and to be considerate of their desires. Then these strange people used plates, knives, forks and spoons, the necessity for which Konah could not comprehend. Are white men's hands so dirty that they do not eat with them? Is one hand used to cut with, the other to shovel with? were queries that passed through her mind.

Thought of such things was soon dissipated by a matter of more immediate interest. A lump of sugar was handed to a woman who was standing at the end of a row of natives. She took the lump, drew her tongue across it in one long delicious lick, and passed it on to her neighbor. Here the performance was repeated, and the sugar passed on down the line, becoming visibly smaller at every exchange. It disappeared entirely just before it reached the end of the line, and the last man was compelled to content himself with licking the fingers that had last held the sweetness.

After the dinner was over, some of the people, thinking that the interesting part of the show was ended, went away, but Konah and many others had no thought of going. Emboldened by the gentle voice and kindly smile of the white women, Konah drew near, touched the soft hands, and examined the dress, but most she wondered at the wealth of wavy hair in such contrast with the short kinky covering of her own curly pate. The missionary, seeing that not only the child, but many of the women as well were deeply interested, graciously undid her hair, and as it tumbled down, a wavy flood, reaching far below her waist, amazed ejaculations burst from the beholders, and excited gesticulations gave expression to feelings for which they could not find words. When the first ecstasy of wonder was over, Konah put out her hand timidly, and drew the soft hair through her fingers. But the missionary, who had learned to look through the eyes down into the soul, had marked Konah as one of those peculiarly bright and promising beings sometimes found in darkest surroundings.

Calling the interpreter, she learned all she could about the child, told her about the mission school, and asked her to come there and be taught all the wonders the white people know. Konah was deeply interested, and more than anxious to go, but of course the question was not hers to decide. Sobah and Mamenah were not so easily persuaded, though they were so far impressed by the first interview as to consent to further palaver on the same subject after the evening service.

The time of the evening meeting found a crowd of two or three hundred people assembled; the organ was again played, a prayer of tender sympathy was offered, and then the magic lantern was brought into use. This created another sensation, and held the audience as under a spell, as picture after picture was thrown upon the canvas, representing the life and the crucifixion of the Saviour of men. At the same time, that simple yet extraordinary life-story was told, with all its display of love and self-sacrifice for the good of others. It was a doctrine absolutely new and incomprehensible to the natives, who knew only the law of self-interest, yet some glimmerings of this new and gentler light began to break in upon their minds, and to send touches of warmth into their hearts.

It was evident that Sobah had been impressed with the events of the day and evening, so after the meeting adjourned, the missionaries went to the appointed conference with renewed hope.

The palaver was long and earnest. Sobah craved the opportunity to investigate new things, and the offer of employment in connection with the mission boats was very attractive, yet it is no easy matter to break with the environments and habits of a lifetime. Besides, procrastination is part of the life of the black man, and so the final decision was postponed until morning. After the missionaries went away to their lodgings, some of their native helpers remained, at Konah's urgent request, to talk further of life at the mission school. Countless were the questions asked and answered.

"Oh," said the girl, who was giving the information, "dey talk de God-word, dey show plenty picture, dey make we sabbee book, learn we fo' sew clo'es, en—" as an inspiration came to her, "dey pull story."

This was a delightful prospect indeed, and Konah, much elated, wanted to know what kind of stories such people told. This is the sample that was given her.

## The New Version Of Eve And The Apple.

"Fus' tem people no bin deh nah de wuld. God say make we pull (create) one man lek we. So he pull one man en one ooman. So nar heah God's people wey he pull. He pull de garden fo' um too. He pull every t'ing fo' den yeat, but one tree he say make yo' no yeat. Satan sen' snake fo' tempt um. De snake walker up lek pusson. He say: 'God story 'pon yo'; yo' no go die; make yo' yeat de fruit.' Den de ooman go pick de plum en yeat um. Den de ooman go tell de man, he say: 'De fruit sweet, make yo' come yeat um.' Den de man come pick de plum en yeat um. Ebenin' tem God bring de light en go look fo' dem, en dey go hide under one tree. God call, dey no answer, but God fine um en say: 'Dat fruit I say make yo' no yeat, yo' bin yeat um?'

"Dey say: 'Yes, one man come en say make we yeat um.'

"Den God punish de people. He say ef dis ooman born pickin, de snake go bite pickin foot. Den God punish de snake. He say w'en de ooman go walker, he no see de snake, he step 'pon heen head en mas' um flat. Nar dat to Mary, Christ's mudder."

The story seemed to Konah much like the ones she loved so well, except that it introduced characters of which she had not heard until that very day. There were questions she was burning to ask regarding the God who had been mentioned so often that day. The visitors undertook to enlighten her. They represented Him as a being who is always kind, and gentle, and helpful, a willing burden bearer for others.

"God he get big cottah (head-pad) so he kin kare all trouble fo' we," was the striking way in which the last truth was expressed. The large cottah, or head-pad, told Konah plainly that this being was accustomed to carry excessive burdens, but that those should be carried "fo' we," she could only partly understand. Going on with his personal experience, the speaker said: "De goodness of de Lawd toward me, my mout' too narrow fo' talk. I no know how fo' 'press dis tankee of God; he done die fo' we, he get up in t'ree day, he go do good fo' we, he no fo'get we. Ef I holler it no sufficien'. Ef it outside matter, my tongue kin ring lek bell, inside it kin tangle en humbug."

A little later the visitors withdrew, and Konah, carried by her eagerness to the very height of presumption, ventured even to make a direct and final appeal to her father, "Oh, Daddy, make we go."

The father had not yet settled the question, so he commanded curtly: "Shut mout'."

Morning came, and with it Sobah's decision to remove to the mission town. Konah was in ecstasy. The people of the village gathered to see the visitors off. As a special mark of friendship Sobah got under one corner of a hammock, and toted it for some distance. Konah was drawn irresistibly to the side of the woman who had put a new warmth into her heart, and a new hope into her life. Lacking the ability to communicate in words, the woman put out her hand. The girl seized it eagerly, and trotted along contentedly by the side of the hammock. Encouraged by Konah's example, other little girls came up and took hold of the hand. Then the other hand was put out, and soon there were as many little girls attached as there were fingers on the hands. They trotted along, laughing and uttering frantic little ejaculations of joy. Whenever a tree crowded too close upon the path, they would loosen their hold, bound around the obstruction, and come back with a cry. So the procession moved on until the river was reached. There the little girls reluctantly halted. Konah stood watching, filled with an intense longing, as the path turned from the further bank of the river, and she saw the last hammock disappear around the bend. Her little heart fluttered with emotion, and her whole childish being reached out from that borderland of darkness, in a mute appeal to be taken along into that warmer, richer light toward which she felt herself drawn by an irresistible attraction. Thus she stood within the shadow, waiting for the coming of the sunshine.

The End.

# VOCABULARY

| | |
|---|---|
| Aintee? | Is it not so? |
| Beef | animals. |
| Betty | better. |
| Bin deh | am or was there. |
| Blow | breathe. |
| Bug-a-bug | *White Ants, Termes Bellicosus.* |
| Bly | basket. |
| Bootoo | stoop, crouch. |
| Calabas' | gourd. |
| Cham | chew. |
| Conk | strike. |
| Cumpin | companion. |
| Deh | there. |
| Dem | they, them, their. |
| Den | they, their, them, then. |
| Do' | door. |
| Do yah | please. |
| Duh | do (auxiliary). |
| Grap | get up. |
| Greedy | begrudge. |
| Hangry | hungry, famine. |
| Hāse | hoist, raise. |
| Hebe | raise, throw. |
| He, heen, him | his. |
| Hō'se | house. |
| Hush yah | term of condolence. |
| Leelee | little. |
| Lek | like, as. |
| Lef | leave, left. |
| Mate | an associate—wife. |
| Nah | at, from, in, on, to. |
| Nar | is, are, was. |
| Net | night. |

| | |
|---|---|
| No mo' | nothing more, merely. |
| Oonah | you. |
| Pin | place, put down. |
| Pickin | pickaninny. |
| Pull | create, tell. |
| Ress | rice. |
| Sabbee | know. |
| San'-san' | sand. |
| Sebbeh | charm. |
| Shabe | divide. |
| Soso | merely. |
| Sotáy | until. |
| 'Tan' | stand. |
| Tay | until, for, a long time. |
| Tem | time. |
| 'Tick | tree, stick. |
| Wey | what, which, who, where, since. |
| Yase | ears. |
| Yi | eye. |

# FOOTNOTES

[1] Wa'm fiah, *i.e.* warm themselves by the fire.

[2] These words represent the sound made by sharpening the axe.

[3] Sotáy he trow 'way nah groun', *i.e.* until it overflows upon the ground.

[4] Puttah-puttah, *i.e.* black mud deposited upon the banks of rivers or pools.

[5] *i.e.*, It is play; I am playing; I am merely playing.

[6] *i.e.*, There was no chance for improvement. It was a hopeless case.

[7] "Heen" refers to Deer. The proposal to wrestle with the little child appeared foolish in the Deer's estimation.

[8] "Long tem" is usually, as in this case, the equivalent of a long time ago. The remote past, rather than duration, is intended.

[9] "Done use me too much," *i.e.* He is too accustomed to me.

[10] "No deny," *i.e.* Do not doubt his ability.

[11] When into the darkness of a mud hut the first rays of dawn penetrate sufficiently to afford from within a clear-cut outline of the door-way, the time is designated by "do' clean."

[12] "So-so san'-san' lef' no mo'," *i.e.* merely sand was left, nothing more. The fire kindled by the terrible combat had consumed everything combustible. This is a characteristic African hyperbole. See also the much exaggerated statement of the space covered by the combat, and of the

size of the cup that each animal was required to empty at one draught.

[13] "Do," often accompanied by a low cringing inclination of the body and clasped hands, is a very strong form of entreaty.

[14] The use of America and England, in the comparison, comes from the vaguest possible conception of those countries, derived in this instance, it may be supposed, from information picked up by Sobah during his visits to Freetown. The series, America, England and Freetown, is intended to form a climax.

[15] This is a characteristic circumlocution. It means that the goat is not scratching, but is swimming, as he did a long time ago.

[16] "He no bin 'tan' lek," *i.e.* Did not stand like, did not appear as he does.

[17] "He gie um four, four," *i.e.* He gave four to each.

[18] To better insure their safety against invading tribes, the people live in villages, often mud-walled, and go at day-break to their farms, where a hut, or a thatched roof supported by poles, serves as temporary abode and shelter. In order to indulge undisturbed his inordinate appetite, Spider plans to be left alone at night upon his farm, when the other members of the household return to the village.

[19] "He no 'tay agin," *i.e.*, It did not stay, was a short time.

[20] The country-fashion man is a sort of African seer, who seats himself upon the ground, spreads a white cloth in front of him, throws upon it small stones and bits of various things, and in some way from these makes his predictions, fumbling in an apparently aimless way, and

muttering to himself, or to the spirits of darkness with which he claims to be in communion. This is about as much as the uninitiated and curious can learn in regard to "Looking the ground."

[21] The wax referred to exudes from a tree called by the natives "chockooh." It is very tenacious.

[22] "'Tick-'poon" *i.e.* a stick used as a substitute for a spoon.

[23] "Hush yah," or "as-yah," is the strongest expression of sympathy in the Sierra Leone dialect.

[24] "Wey t'ing do de place far so?" *i.e.*, Why is the place so far?

[25] To an African mind, everything in the least unusual needs to be accounted for. Consequently some solution, however fanciful, must be offered for the slow locomotion of such a pompous appearing character in the native stories as the Chameleon. Raising one foot after the other slowly, very slowly, he puts it down with a meditative precision that leads the people to ascribe to him these words: "I duh walker, mash (take) one step, den odder step. Ef I walker hard I go sink de groun', de groun' go bus', he too sof', en bimeby de wuld go broke. Dat make I duh walker soffle, so I no fa' down."

[26] Native lack of management, and shiftlessness in providing for the future by planting a sufficient amount of rice, cause, for the great mass of the people, an annual scarcity of food just preceding the season of ingathering. Add to this the frequent wars, and the occasional devastations by locusts, and the explanation is afforded for the famines so frequently mentioned in the oral literature concerning the animals, the pathetic sharers in the suffering of their human friends.

[27] The native rope is a vine that grows in the jungle, and which is sufficiently strong to serve the purposes of a rope. Fastened to a large stone it even holds a boat at anchor.

[28] "Put Bundo" signifies to initiate into the mysteries of the Bundo, a powerful secret organization for women.

[29] The initiation lasts for several weeks, during which period the candidates are not allowed to mingle with the people of the town. A supply of food is therefore necessary, and it is this supply that Spider asks the chief to provide.

[30] The native jug for storing palm-oil, is a joint of bamboo, stopped up at both ends, or a gourd.

[31] The customary way for the chief to issue a proclamation is to send a town crier around, after the people have gathered in the town for the night.

[32] "Pull de Bundo" signifies a public display just after initiation, a procession with songs and dances. For this purpose special and numerous ornaments, and gaudy but scant covering are worn on the partially nude bodies, which are tattooed and greased until they shine.

By the query: "Which side yo' duh pull de Bundo," the chief implies that the preparatory rites over which Spider has been supposed to preside are at an end, and a statement should be made as to the place where the new members are to be introduced to the public.

[33] "Lock" means merely "close," as no stronger method for securing a door is known than bracing a stick against it. Sometimes a door is only a suspended mat.

[34] The Mory men, or Mohammedans, travel over the country, gaining a living by working on the credulity

of the superstitious folk. They manufacture "sebbys" or charms, of which the most common are bits of Arabic writing, usually taken from the Koran, and enclosed in black leather of square or oblong shape, measuring an inch or two. These charms are worn around neck, wrists or ankles.

Natives will sacrifice almost any other possession to procure such charms. Their awed faith in the potency of charms and fetiches is one of the most dumbly pathetic facts in African life.

[35] The cutlass is the general purpose tool used for cutting away underbrush, for harvesting, and even for the felling of forest trees.

[36] "Humbug" in the Sierra Leone dialect always means "trouble", and contains no suggestion of trickery. The thought here is: Let the person give himself no trouble.

[37] The following account of how Mr. Spider cooks his rice before he goes to capture the animal from which he makes the stew for the rice, is an exaggerated illustration of the African tendency to allow each hour to provide for its need. The custom, however, is to cook the rice, set it aside to steam under a grass-woven cover, until the stew is made, and finally to wash the calabashes, *i. e.* gourds which serve as bowls for food and water. Usually eating from the pot dispenses with the last part of the ceremony.

[38] A circular pad worn upon the head when "toting" a hammock or other burden.

[39] Beard.

[40] "No able um", *i. e.* Was not able to surpass him.

[41] The prophet bird is about the size of a hummingbird.

It utters notes which are believed to indicate danger or success, especially when heard at the beginning of a journey, or just preceding the beginning of some task. The sounds from the tiny throat are sufficient to reverse the best laid plans, or to establish greater confidence in them.

[42] The accent falls upon the first syllable of the verb, the pronunciation being the same as that of the noun.

[43] For explanation of "half side," see Introduction, page 21.

[44] The man's house signifies the hut assigned to him by the chief on his arrival in the town. This custom supplies the lack of hotels.

[45] Craw-craw is a very prevalent skin disease, a species of itch not very contagious.

[46] When the men choose to clothe themselves further than with the customary loin cloth, they wear a long loose gown of hand-spun and woven cloth. Often this has a large pocket sewed on the front.

[47] The kola is eaten to still the pangs of hunger, and because an appetite for it is easily acquired. Then its intense bitterness becomes sweet. The white kolas are slightly preferred to the pink, either being given as a token of friendship and hospitality.

[48] One country cloth is thought to be sufficient bed for anyone. The evident purpose of the little boy in asking for a "pile" of clothes is to give the devil a task requiring much time, in order to delay his designs against the young woman.

[49] "Trongah yase," *i.e.*, "strong ears," wilful disregard of advice.

[50] "Wey t'ing dat?" *i.e.* What (thing) is that?

[51] See footnote page 240.

[52] See footnote page 47.

[53] See footnote page 100.

[54] The coal referred to is charcoal. The natives know nothing of the natural product.

[55] "De bigness of he foot," *i. e.* leg. In the dialect the foot and hand may include the leg and arm, there being no distinctive terms for each.

[56] A barreh is a public meeting-place. A town has one or more, according to the population. It consists of a mud floor surrounded by a wall two or three feet high, and covered by a projecting grass or palm thatch. It is absolutely devoid of furnishings, unless there may be a hammock, or one or two bamboo stools, occasionally a crude chair, made of peculiarly forked sticks.

[57] "Dey mine um sotay he begin use dem," *i.e.* The boys cared for the animal until it became accustomed to them.

[58] The mortar and pestle are used in all homes for beating rice. The fanners are flat woven trays, on which the rice, after it is pounded, is shaken to remove the chaff.

[59] A common sight among the natives is a little child busily engaged in picking the lice from the woolly head of some older person. Sometimes the child's place is taken by the pet monkey. If the monkey fails to find the object of his search, he loses his temper, and expresses his feelings in strong language, and in boxing the person's head.

[60] 'It will not be my fault if anybody is killed.'

[61] "Palm-ile" is the general term meaning fat or oil of any kind.

[62] The Manekky society is a secret organization for murdering the infirm and the incurable.

[63] "'Tronger yase" *i.e.*, strong ears, obstinacy.

[64] Watch-pot is the usual expression for a protracted call, the chief aim of which is to remain until the next meal is prepared and served. Such a stay has an air of deliberation about it, something like taking one's knitting and remaining for tea.

[65] The "clo'es" were pieces of cloth for the customary present, which the stranger offers as indirect payment for the hospitality he expects to receive.

[66] As soon as a death is reported, the people gather around the corpse, and, prone upon the ground, indulge in the wildest lamentations and cries. This duty is especially incumbent upon the women, and their wailing and grovelling, accompanied by writhings and contortions of the body, must be something like the death-wail of the lost.

[67] Coffins are unknown to native life. The dead are wrapped in white cloth and grass woven mamats and laid in shallow graves.

[68] The place of burial for a baby, especially if it be the first, is usually a refuse heap, the belief being that if the child is too deeply mourned and honored, the parents will have no more offspring. A second child is buried nearer the house; while the most honorable interment given an older person, is within the house. The "bush" and the road-side, receive the majority of the dead.

# TRANSCRIBER'S NOTE

Obvious printer errors have been corrected. Otherwise, the author's original spelling, punctuation and hyphenation have been left intact.

www.ingramcontent.com/pod-product-compliance
Lightning Source LLC
Chambersburg PA
CBHW071835020726
47502CB00004B/1366

* 9 7 8 1 6 3 6 5 2 2 4 8 7 *